Sal
family is everything
[signature] x

FLAGRANT

An Inferno World Novel

ALLY VANCE

CW01551458

Editor: Sheena Taylor
Formatting: Pink Elephant Designs
Cover Design: Pretty in Ink Creations

INFERNO SERIES

Sparks by Yolanda Olson
Inferno by Yolanda Olson
Cinere by Yolanda Olson
Embers by Yolanda Olson
Inferno Series Boxset by Yolanda Olson
Scorched by Yolanda Olson & Jennifer Bene

INFERNO WORLD BOOKS

Verboten by A. A. Davies
Malignus by Dani René
Iniquity by Emery LeeAnn
Obloquy by Murphy Wallace
Burned by Jennifer Bene
Flagrant by Ally Vance
Cognati by K Webster writing as Elizabeth Gray
Desiccate by Charity B.
Simmer by Measha Stone

To Yolanda, who inspired every word across these pages, thank you for bringing me into your world. Love Ally
#TheOriginalDaddysGirl

Have we forgot it's your blood inside of my veins that feeds my heart
Tyrant, Immortalized, Disturbed, 2015.

Playlist

Tyrant by Disturbed

Prologue

I've never known my daddy's love. My mom did everything she could to keep me safe from the man she deemed a monster. She knew I wanted to find him, so she persisted in her refusal to divulge even the smallest scrap of information to assist me in my search. All she could ever bring herself to tell me was that I had his smile and his eyes, and when she sliced open her veins from wrist to elbow, two days before my eighteenth birthday, she took the secret of his identity with her to the grave.

In spite of my mom's blatant fear of him, the unrelenting need to know exactly who my father is and where I come from never fades. He's a nameless, faceless entity, more like a myth than a man, and given my mom's desperate craving for secrecy where he's concerned, I doubt he's aware I exist.

I'm going to find him, and it doesn't matter if he

knows about me or not. I want to meet the man who helped to create me. Mom didn't want this for me, but she made her decision when she chose to leave behind the shattered fragments of our broken family: a daughter and a daddy who've both been kept in the dark about each other. I'm not afraid of the dark, though. I'm more afraid of the loneliness hiding within the shadows.

Chapter One

Shortly after the funeral, when my stepdad, Gregory, is out of the house, I slip into his and mom's bedroom to look for even the smallest of clues about my real daddy. There's no love lost between me and Gregory. He's an alcoholic and an abusive asshole who can't keep his hands to himself even when he's sober. I never told Mom about his inappropriate behavior; there was no point. Apart from getting a little handsy with me and some leers that make my skin crawl, he's never taken it any further.

I find a box full of photographs and papers in the bottom of Mom's closet, and a quick rifle through the contents tells me instantly that it belonged to her. Listening carefully to check the house is still silent, I make sure everything in the bedroom looks undisturbed and hurry back to my room with the heavy box clutched tightly to my chest, trying not to drop it.

I place the box on my bed before shutting and locking my bedroom door. I don't want Gregory poking his head in here; he's been awful since Mom died, and he hovers around me even more than he did before. I want to get out of here, and as soon as I find any sign or whisper of where my daddy could be, I'm gone.

Carefully, I pry off the lid and pull out handfuls of papers and a stack of photographs and begin flicking through them. A tear falls as I pause on one of me and Mom pulling silly faces at the camera. There was no note, no explanation as to why she felt she had no other choice than to do what she did. She left me all alone. I have nothing of hers except Gregory and a box filled with memories. Wiping away the tears from my eyes, I continue to dig through the contents. There are lots of photos of me and Mom from years ago, and some of her with her friends, when she was about the age I am now. I roll my eyes at all the paperwork and skim through it, not expecting to find anything, until I notice a sheet that makes me drop everything I'm holding in shock.

Heart racing, I grab up the official looking document and read it, once, twice, three times. It's my birth certificate, but the name is wrong, it says Sofia *Greene*. I rifle through some more of the papers, and find a re-registry certificate dated a month later to change my surname to Richards, which is Mom's last name. I knew Mom had kept things hidden from me, but I never imagined that included the fact she changed my name. Why was it so important to her to keep this a secret? There's no way my real daddy could be any worse than wandering hands Gregory. I laugh hollowly, tears forming in my eyes as I stare down at the name *Greene* written in Mom's neat cursive. I think I just found out my daddy's family name. My surname isn't Richards, it's Greene, and I'm taking it back.

I keep looking through the box but find nothing else of interest. I glance back down at the birth certificate again and notice the name of the hospital I was born in and the address where Mom was living at the time. The town mentioned is not too far from here; it's maybe half a day away, traveling on foot. I have an address, a name, and a legacy I know nothing about. It's a start, but I'm determined to find out more, and I know I need to leave now before Gregory comes home, or otherwise, he'll stop me from going.

I'm just about to throw everything back into the box when I notice a small envelope lying on the bed. Opening it, I see that it contains several more photographs. The first one I take out is of Mom when she was only a little older than I am now. She's standing in a forest and smiling shyly at the camera. The next is of a large stone house with trees framing it and a truck parked out front. Lastly, there's a photo of a man, and my heart stutters unevenly in my chest the longer I stare at it. There's something about him that captures my attention, and I'm unable to look away from his image. Heat coils in my stomach at the way his dark eyes seem to penetrate my soul even from a photograph, and I hungrily rake my eyes over the rest of him, devouring everything the small picture has to offer.

Forcing myself to look away, I slide the photos back into the envelope along with the documents relating to my birth. Finally, I select a couple more of my favorite pictures from Mom's box and add them in as well. I'll take them all with me when I leave. Grabbing a large backpack from my closet, I shove in a few sets of clothes, making sure I have thick socks and sweaters in case it gets cold. I have very little money, so I'll be camping. I'm just glad I've a small tent and sleeping bag, left over from my girl scout days, I can use. It'll beat sleeping completely exposed to the elements.

I've no trinkets I want to take with me; there's nothing of value that I hold dear. The only thing I cared about was Mom, and she's sleeping in the earth now. I throw on a thick jacket, haul my back-pack onto my shoulders, and pick up the tent. I'll quickly grab some food and water from the kitchen on my way out and be gone by the time Gregory returns.

I go over to my bedroom door, and turning the key, the lock clicks loudly as it releases. Steeling myself for what I'm about to do, I pull the door open and let out a scream when I see Gregory swaying unsteadily on the other side, smelling strongly of cheap whiskey and cigarette smoke.

He breathes the putrid scent of booze all over my face as he reaches out and grabs my upper arm in his meaty hand.

"Where do you think you're going, Fia?" he slurs.

Chapter Two

Gregory's hand tightens around my arm when I try to wrench it away. The stench of his breath combined with the underlying smell of sweat is a toxic mixture, and it takes everything in me not to retch. I hate when he calls me Fia; it's what Mom used to call me, only the way she said it never made my skin crawl and my stomach threaten to rebel.

"Out. I'm going to a friend's house for a sleepover," I lie, looking at him directly.

I don't dare trip on my words or betray myself with a falter in my expression.

"No, you're not," he slurs, squeezing my arm tighter and swaying unsteadily.

I grab the door frame to stop myself from stumbling when he uses his full weight to pull me toward him in an uncoordinated movement.

"Gregory, let go of me. You're hurting my arm," I tell him, forcing myself to keep a level tone.

Panic is rising, he's never been quite so firm with me before, not physically at least.

"How many times have I told you that I don't like it when you call me Gregory?" he growls, his words running together almost unintelligibly.

I try and fail to suppress a shudder of revulsion, but thankfully, he doesn't notice.

"Mom always called you by your name, and she never told me I had to call you anything else."

"Well, I remember telling you when I married your mom that you could call me 'Dad'. After all, your real daddy was a real piece of work. No wonder your mom left him just after they found out she was pregnant with you. She told him she'd miscarried. He'd never have let her go otherwise." His words are clearer now, the slur beginning to fade.

Anger bubbles furiously inside me at his words, and I feel his barb about my real daddy stabbing me to the heart. I want to find out the truth for myself, but I'd rather face my 'real daddy' who 'was a piece of work' than stay here with Gregory another minute. He's a sleaze, and at this point, I've little doubt that he'd garner some sick satisfaction out of having me call him 'Dad'.

"I'm going out. I'll see you later," I reaffirm the lie and wait for him to let go.

Drunk or not, Gregory isn't a weak man, and I've always been on the more petite size; I'm sure it wouldn't take much for him to overpower me, not that it would stop me from fighting back. One of the reasons Mom called me Fia was because when we argued I'd refuse to back down. I've always been stubborn and fiery, just like she was.

I'm surprised Gregory isn't grilling me for every detail of where I'm planning to stay, and I'm relieved he doesn't seem to have noticed how much stuff I'm taking with me for a sleepover. He must be more inebriated than usual.

I flex my arm, testing his hold, and he tightens his grip, momentarily, before releasing me.

"I want you back by midnight, Fia, no sleeping over," Gregory barks, and I fight the urge to roll my eyes at him.

"Sure, I'll be back by midnight," I agree, but it's an empty promise.

I'm never coming back to this place. I've got everything I need packed in the backpack I'm taking with me. There's nothing left for me here. Mom is gone, and this house is a black hole formed of negative energy and the overbearing presence of Gregory.

He staggers off down the hallway to his and Mom's bedroom, and I let out a heavy sigh of relief. I was expecting that to go a lot worse than it did, but it seems like I worried for nothing. I make my way along the upstairs hallway, and I'm just about to head down the stairs when a shout of fury stops me in my tracks.

"Fia!" Gregory roars, storming toward me with anger blazing in his alcohol-glazed eyes and a fistful of photographs clenched in his fist.

Shit! I must have missed them when I had a brief look through Mom's box while in her closet. Even with his fat thumb covering our faces, I can see there's a photo of Mom and me on top. I hitch my bag up higher on my shoulder and dart down the stairs, taking the steps two at a time. I don't want to wait to see what he's going to do. He knows I've been in their room and going through Mom's stuff. I have every right to search through her things and look at those photos, but clearly he doesn't agree.

"Leave me alone!" I scream as he comes hurtling unsteadily down the stairs with the promise of punishment in his eyes.

He scares me when he gets like this, transforming into someone I don't recognize. It doesn't happen often, but when it does, someone always gets hurt, and it's usually me. Without Mom to calm his drunken rage, I've no way of knowing just how bad it's going to get. I've got to get out of here.

Reaching the front door, I fumble with the lock, cursing when I realize I've needlessly wasted precious seconds because the drunken fool hasn't engaged the latch and chain. Yanking on the door, it begins to open just as the meaty hand of Gregory slams it back into its frame. I let out a squeal of shock, and dropping to the floor, I crawl away as fast as I can, frustrated at how the tent, sleeping bag, and backpack are weighing me down.

The bags containing the camping supplies prove to be my undoing, and I'm prevented from getting away when Gregory uses them to haul me back. I've no choice but to shrug the bags off my shoulder to escape him while making sure to keep hold of my backpack; I'm not leaving that behind. Crawling forward as best I can from my position on the floor, I duck beneath his clumsy grab at me, and sprint for the back door and salvation.

"Fia! Get your ass back here. Explain yourself. What were you doing in my bedroom?" he bellows, and I can hear his heavy footsteps pounding on the floor as he follows after me. "You're not going anywhere, little girl!"

I'm not going to stop and explain myself to him. It's not like he'd listen, and there's no way in hell I'm going to stick around to watch his rage explode with the same force as a small bomb detonating. He's a mean ass drunk, and the only person who could snap him out of it was Mom. But Mom's gone, and I'm alone. I want nothing to do with Gregory. As far as I'm concerned, he's never been my family. He could fall off a cliff and I wouldn't shed a tear for the bastard. I reach the back door, and pulling it open, I bolt for freedom and a future that can only be an improvement on the one I'm leaving behind.

Chapter Three

Positioning my backpack more securely on my shoulders, I keep moving. My feet ache, and it's getting darker. I've been walking for hours and the long stretch of road seems to be endless. Lush woodland grows on either side, creating a thin canopy overhead. I lost the camping supplies in the scuffle with Gregory, so either I'm going to have to rough it without a shelter or ask someone for help. Looking around, I think it's probably going to be the former.

When it gets too dark to see, I drop into a crouch, and pulling off my backpack, I rummage inside, feeling for a flashlight. My hand closes around the long metal handle, and having extracted it, I flick the switch on. I should've stopped sooner, but the farther away from home I travel, the better I feel. Only now, I can't see shit, and I've got to find some shelter in the pitch black in the middle of fucking nowhere.

My stomach rumbles, and I curse Gregory for his ridiculously bad timing, coming home when he did. In my hurry to get away, not only did I lose the tent but also never grabbed any food or water to bring with me. Given my lack of shelter, light, and sustenance, I decide it's probably safer to keep going rather than remain here and search in the dark for somewhere to sleep.

As I walk, I ponder on what I've learned about myself. I knew Gregory wasn't my real dad; he came into Mom's life after I was born, but finding out that the name I've carried all these years is a lie was a big shock, and it's given me hope. I'm not sure who or what I'll discover when I reach my destination, but at the very least I may get some answers. Even if I find nothing, I'm going to build myself a new life away from the memories. After narrowly escaping from Gregory, I don't dare go back there anyway. With no one to take his anger out on, it's only going to fester and grow before exploding uncontrollably, and I don't want to be around when it does. A prickle of sadness snags at my heart at the few happy memories I'm leaving behind, but in recent years, the bad ones far outweigh the good.

I've hardly taken a break all night, but even though I've carried on moving, I've slowed my pace. I'm not stupid and didn't want to have an accident and hurt myself in the dark. The rising sun turns the sky a pinkish-red hue, and I take in the pretty spread of light skimming across the wispy clouds. I let out a heavy sigh and force my legs to keep going, but I'm sluggish with exhaustion and making very little progress. I've not eaten or drunk anything since yesterday, and I haven't slept at all in over twenty-four hours.

Relief floods through me as I turn a sharp bend in the road and see my destination ahead, finally. A last burst of energy surges through me, giving me a second wind, and I slowly jog down the hill into the town. I just make it to the bottom when I hear the sound of a truck approaching from the other direction. Just in time, I dodge out of the way, landing in the shallow ditch by the side of the road. I manage to catch a glimpse of the driver as he passes unapologetically by, and I frown when he continues on his journey without stopping. *Fucker nearly killed me.* Shaking my head, I carry on into town.

By the time I finally arrive at the town, I'm completely famished, so I head to the nearest cafe for coffee and some breakfast. It doesn't take long before I'm digging into a delicious, freshly toasted bagel, lightly spread with butter, and a coffee that's both hot and rejuvenating. I needed this. I order a second helping of both and before long they're gone too, and I'm feeling so much better.

As I begin my third cup of coffee, I pull the

photos from my backpack and stare at them. The picture of Mom with me when I was young makes my heart ache, and the longer I look at it, the more it hurts…I miss her so much. I slam it face down on the table, ignoring the glowering looks from a couple of elderly women at the neighboring table. Next, I pick up the one of the man; it draws me in like a black hole. I sip at my coffee while transfixed by the dark eyes penetrating me from a mere photograph. My breath catches in my chest, and I swallow hard against the pressure, gulping down air. I'm here to find my daddy, but the longer I stare at the photo, taking in the ruggedly handsome features, the neat black hair, and the slight smirk that makes me want to squirm in my seat, the less I want to find those answers, and the more I just want to find *him*.

My head is spinning by the time I manage to tear my gaze away from his face. The remnants of my coffee are cold, and the older women from the next table are gone. *How long have I been sitting here?* I glance up at the clock and realize I've been here for over an hour and have spent virtually the whole time staring at the image of the stranger from my mom's past. Getting up, I feel the ache in my legs return. I'm almost hobbling as I make my way to the counter to pay and ask for directions to the address listed on my birth certificate.

Destination and directions firmly in mind, I

repeat them over and over as I walk the distance on tired, aching legs, letting my determination and the coffee be the fuel that carries me onward. After what seems like forever and feeling close to dropping where I stand, I arrive at an old house with the faded number I'm looking for displayed on its worn, wooden front door. Taking a deep breath, I slowly venture through the gate to the property and down the path that's sprouting weeds between the paved slabs. By the time I reach the doorstep with a cracked flowerpot next to it, my heart is pounding. I hope I can find some of the answers I'm looking for, otherwise this journey will have been for nothing.

I knock on the door and wait. After a few moments, the door opens and an elderly lady appears and stands in the shadows at the threshold. She moves closer, and my heart sinks when I realize she's an older version of Gregory. She even has the same murkiness to her eyes, and the familiar stench of alcohol and cigarettes wafts from her.

"Aren't you Kayley Richards little girl? You're the spitting image of her. My worthless son left his momma behind to go and raise you. What the hell are you doing on my property? I don't want you here," she hurls out at me, and I take a step back in alarm.

"I-I came here to find out who my real daddy is. S-Sorry, I'm going to go," I stammer.

A knowing look crosses the old woman's face,

and her eyes narrow on me before her lips twist up into a wide smile, revealing yellowed, cracked teeth. Inwardly shuddering, I go to take another step back, but she lunges out, and grabbing my arm with a fierce, bony grip, she drags me into her fetid house, locking the door behind us.

Chapter Four

The farther into the house I'm dragged, the more I want to hack up a lung like a pack-a-day smoker because that's exactly how I feel when breathing in the stale, smoky air.

"I'll go. You don't have to bring me in here. I didn't mean to disturb you," I cough, testing her hold and trying to resist her, but the old bat is stronger than she looks.

"Nonsense, you're *family*," she chides, drawing out the word family in a way that raises goosebumps all over my skin.

She relentlessly tugs me along behind her and takes me to one of the most depressing sitting rooms I've ever seen. The walls are stained yellow with age and years of cigarette smoke, and the whole room is dank and dingy. I feel sick, but I'm not entirely sure it's only because of the smell. A heavy sense of dread has settled over me like a layer of dust, and I want to choke on it all.

"Sit," she rasps in a thick tone, and I glance at the old couch that's seen better days before reluctantly settling on the very edge of the seat.

Letting out an impatient huff at my hesitance, she shakes her head before shuffling across the room to a phone so old it's practically obsolete. She picks up the receiver and dials a number. I can't hear what she's saying in a hushed tone with the TV playing in the background, but the repeated glances she keeps sending my way put me even more on edge.

Once the call ends, she leaves me and walks into her kitchen, situated across the hallway from where I'm sitting. Through the open doorways, I can see her watching me like a hawk eyeing up its prey, and my skin crawls with unease. It takes what seems like an age for her to boil a kettle and come back through with three mugs of coffee on a tray. We haven't spoken in several minutes.

"Are you expecting company?" I ask, desperately seeking an excuse to get out of here as soon as possible, preferably before I have to drink what she's prepared for us.

"No," she replies, but I sense that she's not being truthful.

She carefully places each of the mugs on stained coasters. She didn't ask me if I wanted a coffee or how I like it, but I can safely say it's not the way she's prepared it for me. She sits down in a worn out, sagging armchair opposite me and lifts her mug to her lips.

"Drink," she insists, gesturing at the coffee sitting untouched in front of me.

I don't want to drink it, but I don't think she's about to let me out of here any time soon, and the longer I sit staring with disdain and dismay at the hideous looking offering in front of me, the worse I can tell it's going to be. Reluctantly, I lift the mug to my lips and take a mouthful. The hot liquid scalds my tongue, and I can only hope it will dull my sense of taste for the rest of the drink because it tastes vile.

Then I hear something that makes my heart stall and my blood run cold.

"Mom!" Gregory's voice booms through the house in time with the slam of a door, and I jump in my seat, alert and tense.

Shit! The old bat called Gregory, and it sounds like he's actually sober for a change. Without him in his usual inebriated state, he'll be sharper, and I'll have less chance of getting away from him now than I did back at my mom's house.

I'm frozen to the spot. My eyes stare unblinking at the entrance to the hallway as I wait for him to approach. My gaze slips to his mother, and the malice in her expression unfreezes me. I leap to my feet and bolt out of the sitting room. Flying into the hallway, I hope and pray for the element of surprise, but instead crash straight into my stepdad.

He wraps his waiting arms around my body, and I let out a piercing scream as I start to thrash in his hold, trying to kick at any part of him I can reach. His grip doesn't slacken, instead tightening until I feel my ribs start to scream under the pressure and my shouts weaken into a cough as he crushes me against his chest.

"Fia, I've been looking for you. You ran off when I was trying to talk to you," he growls into my ear.

He may be sober, but the stench of alcohol hasn't faded from his breath, and his clothes still bear the unpleasant smell of sweat, booze, and cigarettes. I shouldn't have come here. He takes a step back, bringing me along with him. I dig my heels into the filthy, old hallway carpet but fail to get any purchase and find myself helpless against his superior strength. I wriggle and struggle, digging my nails into his skin, but it's to no avail.

"Stop fighting me, Fia. I just want to talk to you," he bites out, shaking me when I continue to fight.

Taking advantage of the space he's put between us, I slam my knee into his groin. Gregory lets out an agonized grunt and doubles over, knees buckling, but he doesn't relinquish his hold, and I'm pulled down with him, a yelp ripping from my chest as I'm now pinned beneath his weight. Frantically, I try to buck him off, rolling and squirming underneath him.

"Look at the two of you together!" Gregory's mom shouts, her face twisted with a sick glee, and he looks up at her with disgust.

"Mom, how I discipline my stepdaughter is none of your business," he snaps at her, getting to his feet.

She scoffs, "Getting as bad as the rest of the family are you? Tried to fight it, but when Kayley Richards popped out one of our own, I knew you wouldn't be able to resist the pull."

"What?" I gasp, choking on the smell emanating from the carpet that's now too close to my face for comfort.

I drag myself up onto my hands and knees and begin to crawl slowly away from the pair of them.

"Never told ya, did she?" the old bat laughs, the sound reedy and thin.

"Told me what?" I ask, but Gregory cuts her off before she can answer.

"Get out, Mom. I need to talk with my step-daughter," he barks, and reaching down, he grabs me by the ankle and yanks me back toward him.

I yelp and grab hold of one of the wooden posts supporting the banister, but it snaps in my hand, and Gregory continues to drag me by my ankle farther into the house. I viciously kick out at him with my free leg, but when he lets go of me, I crash to the floor. His mom is cackling in the background, and I'm fucking terrified.

"Get that girl under control, Gregory. I'm going to make dinner," she says, clearly bored of watching us grapple with each other while I try desperately to escape from him, and from this house.

"If you leave now, you'll never find out who your daddy is or learn the answers to all those other questions spinning around in that head of yours," Gregory growls, and I hesitate long enough for him to take advantage.

A blow to the back of my head sends me crashing to the floor, and before I black out, I hear the faint raspy voice of Gregory's mom saying, "There was no need to hit her. I drugged her coffee. She'd have been unconscious in another few minutes. Get her upstairs to one of the bedrooms, and for goodness sake make sure she can't escape. Last thing we need is her getting out."

Chapter Five

Voices speaking next to me filter through a haze. My head hurts as I try to focus on their words without letting them know I'm awake.

"You're such an idiot for letting her get this far. What if she'd found him?" Gregory's mom hisses from somewhere near my feet.

My wrists are bound, and I feel vulnerable. Who knows what they did to me while I was unconscious?

"She couldn't have. He's careful not to reveal his whereabouts, and it's not like he'd admit to anyone who he is," Gregory snorts.

"Well, if he somehow discovers what you've done, keeping his daughter from him and now holding her captive, you'd better not bring that shit-storm to my door. When you ran off with Kayley and helped her to conceal the pregnancy, you signed your own damn death certificate. You told him the baby was born dead, yet here she is, all grown up and large as fucking life," she retorts.

"I can handle him, and I can handle her. Neither of them needs to know the truth about each other's existence. Considering his warped idea of the meaning of family, she's better off with me," Gregory snaps.

"Ha! You can barely handle your teenage step-daughter, yet you think you can take on Luke? He got the genes, the strength, the looks...and the dark-ness from the other side of his family," she laughs, wheezing, and descending into a fit of coughing.

"Shut up, you'll wake her," Gregory scolds.

I feel his clammy hand on my neck. His fingers press lightly against the side of my throat, checking my pulse. I force myself to remain still, but I'm sure he must be able to feel my heart racing. The knowl-edge that my family history is within my grasp and that my daddy instils a fearful wariness in my captors sends a thrill through me. I'm fighting not to show any signs of my joy, especially at the thought of Gregory getting his ass handed to him on a platter.

I hear the sound of footsteps getting fainter, moving away from me. The door, to what I assume is a bedroom, creaks loudly before being clicked shut. I'm alone...I hope. I'm too scared to open my eyes and find out. Instinct is telling me that danger still lurks within the room.

A hand touches my leg and I jump.

"I knew you weren't asleep," Gregory mutters, loud enough for me to hear.

I open my eyes, and I'm met with his leering gaze, smirking down at me. I'd scream, but what good would it do when I know the only other person who could hear me won't help.

"Silly girl, just like Kayley. I helped her hide from your daddy after he knocked her up. She told him she miscarried, but it was a lie. He was so angry when she ran. She didn't know what kind of man she'd given herself to. He always was a charming sonofabitch," he laughs, running his hand lightly up and down my leg.

I quiver, my breath escaping in short, sharp pants.

"Let me go, I don't want to know anymore about my mom and daddy."

"Yes, you do. Why else would you be going through your mom's things and turn up here of all places? I think it burns you up inside; the not knowing is eating at your soul, and it's starting to blacken and crumble. You can't stand it," he hisses, gripping my leg tighter until I gasp. "The best part is he doesn't even know you exist, and for the second time in my life, I have something he desperately wants, only this time, he doesn't even know it."

"Stop. Please stop, Mom wouldn't want this," I plead, trying to pull my leg out of his grasp.

My hands are tied to the bed frame, and I'm lying flat on my back, unable to do much except try and kick out, but he's holding me too tightly. As a tear slips from the corner of my eye, his hand continues its journey upward over the denim jeans I'm wearing. He doesn't stop until his hand reaches the juncture of my thighs.

"I wonder how he'd feel if he found out that I got to taste you first? If he knew I got to fuck you hard and fill you up before he had the chance to destroy your virginity with his dick," he mumbles, and I frown in confusion. He must be speaking about someone else.

I can smell the fresh booze on Gregory's breath. He's drunk again, as is the norm with my stepdad. The drink is his mistress, the one thing he loves above all else, even more than my mom when she was alive. His fingers fumble with the zipper on my jeans. When I attempt to twist away, he easily flattens me back down onto the bed with a hand on my stomach, holding me in place. He pulls at my jeans and panties, trying to lower them, but he can't get them down past my hips, and I pray to whatever God there may be that he fails to follow through with his threat.

I'm crying, loud ugly sobs, as he climbs onto the bed, forces my legs as far apart as my clothing will allow, and slides his hand into my panties. He pushes his fat fingers into my dry pussy, and his mouth lands on my clit, sloppily licking at whatever exposed skin he can reach with his foul tongue. When he finally stops, he moves up until his face is in line with mine and frees his limp dick from his pants. I scream, long and loud, as he attempts to get himself hard, and he clamps a hand down over my mouth.

"Shut it, you'll bring my mom back up here," he grits out, words slurring between his bared teeth.

His brow is furrowed in concentration as he tries and fails to get his dick hard. Eventually, he accepts defeat and tucks it away before straightening up.

"Damn, guess fucking the family isn't what gets me going after all. Your taste is sweet, little Greene, just like your momma. Too bad your daddy fucked that relationship up before he could lay his eyes on you," he sneers, staggering from the room, and slamming the door shut behind him.

Chapter Six

As soon I'm alone, I grimace down at my unzipped jeans and partially exposed pussy. There's no way I can escape, and I'm feeling despondent. I know in my heart that my mom wouldn't want me to give up hope, though, and something tells me my daddy would be disappointed too. I shrug off the heaviness threatening to drown me, and angle my head to better see the restraints binding me to the bed in this damned hellhole. It looks like strips of material have been used, and I awkwardly twist my body to reach them with my mouth.

I tug at the material with my teeth, frantically working at the knots. My shoulders and body scream at the pressure from being contorted in such an unnatural angle, but to my delight the knots start to loosen, and I'm able to pull one hand free. Then, getting onto my knees, I untie the other restraint, one-handed.

Once I have both hands free, I quickly tug my jeans into place and fasten them back up, sighing with relief that Gregory failed to violate me as much as he'd initially intended. His comments were confusing; he seemed to be talking about more than one person, but I don't care to know any more. Spying my backpack sitting on top of a chest of drawers, I grab it and sling it over my aching shoulders.

I glance nervously toward the door and then back to the chest, contemplating whether I have enough time to search through it. Deciding to take the risk, I pull the top drawer open but see nothing of interest, just some make-up and an old tarnished hairbrush. Shutting it quietly, I check the other two drawers, one by one, but they're both empty, and I huff out an annoyed breath at the time I've wasted. However, as I shut the final drawer, the sound of paper rustling catches my attention, and frowning, I drop cautiously to my knees and pull it open again to take a closer look. I don't see anything at first, but when I tilt my head to the side, I see an envelope poorly taped to the base of the middle drawer with one word written on it, 'Greene'. I snatch it up, shove it into my backpack, and shut the drawer.

Standing, I turn, and treading as lightly as possible, I head for the door. In a place as old and uncared for as this, there's bound to be a few squeaky floorboards. I pry the door open carefully, and strain my ears to hear what's going on downstairs. The sound of shouting filters up and I use the loud vocals as an opportunity to slip out without giving myself away. I creep down the stairs and pause briefly to eavesdrop on the argument.

"You shouldn't have touched her. You're a fucking fool for daring to lay a hand on that girl. Whatever our blood may be, and whatever cravings may or may not flow through us, I didn't raise you to be a fool. It's bad enough you ran off with his girl and helped her hide the baby, but now you gotta go and fuck it up even more," Gregory's mom angrily scolds, sounding raspier than she did before, probably from all the shouting.

"I didn't fuck her. I couldn't," Gregory counters.

She laughs, "Your limp dick is no concern of mine, and whether you did or not, you put it near what's his and you're gonna pay for that. If he comes looking for you, then you're on your own. Get outta my sight you drunken lout," she finishes, and I hear a door being opened farther along the hallway.

Shit! I hurriedly look around for someplace I can hide, and I spot a hallway closet under the stairs with a broken latch. It's not ideal and probably full of spiders, but I'd take arachnids over Gregory and his mom any day, and this just happens to be the day. Taking a deep breath, I quickly yank the door open and squeeze inside, making sure not to knock anything over in my hurry. Once I'm safely within the closeted space, I reach out and pull the door closed.

My heart is pounding, and pure unadulterated fear floods my veins with ice. At any moment they're going to discover my absence from the bedroom, and I'll have only a few minutes, if I'm lucky, to get the fuck out of this hideous house and away from the family my mom chose for us. I don't have the answers I've come looking for, and I sense that even though Gregory's telling the truth and knows more about my family than I do, it's not worth the price I'd have to pay in exchange for that information.

Considering the number of times Gregory's sneaked a grope in the past, I'm inclined to believe that his impotence was a result of his mom being nearby rather than his own lack of desire. This is the first time he's taken it so far, though, and I pray he never gets the opportunity again. I'll do everything possible to ensure he doesn't ever lay a finger on me now or in the future.

Footsteps on the stairs shake dust loose from the boards above me and I have to stifle a cough. More dust swirls through the air, and my lungs feel tight, and my nose begins to itch with the need to sneeze. I can't stop it; the sneeze erupts from my chest, sounding unreasonably loud within the enclosed space. The footsteps stop and begin a slow descent. I've got no choice, I have to get out, and it has to be now.

I throw the door open and stumble out of the closet as a shout follows after me. I dart through the house and find myself in a small dining room that stinks of cigarettes and looks to be in worse shape than the sitting room. Not stopping, I grab the heaviest object I can find, a small footstool, and I hurl it through the window, shattering it into pieces with a crash.

"Hey! Get back here you little bitch," Gregory's mom curses after me, bursting into the room with him hot on her heels.

I risk one final glance back before following the footstool through the broken window, scratching my arms on the glass as I clamber out and bolt for freedom. I run without pausing until I'm far away from the house, and the shouts of Gregory and his mom have faded into the distance.

Chapter Seven

I have no destination in mind but fear drives me on, urging me to place as much distance as possible between myself and the house I've just escaped from. I shudder inwardly at the memory of Gregory's hands and tongue on me, and moving to the side of the road, I bend over and empty the contents of my stomach into the bushes. From my backpack, I retrieve a bottle of water, purchased earlier at the coffee shop, and quickly rinse out my mouth to remove the sour taste.

Looking around, I realize I'm no longer in the town, and the woodland on each side of the road I'm now walking along is dense and imposing, surrounding me in a sea of green. It's daylight, and the sky is pale, so I'm not sure how long I was unconscious. The old bat drugged me and Gregory knocked me out, so who knows how much time has passed…no more than the rest of the day, surely?

I carry on walking, moving away from the bush that my stomach just greeted and deeper into the forest, looking for somewhere I can stop for a while, undiscovered. I spot a clearing through the trees and head toward it. Hopefully, it'll be a good place to rest up, get my bearings, and maybe read the contents of the envelope that's now safely tucked away in my backpack. I'll also be out of view of the road should Gregory happen to drive past, looking for me.

As I break through the boundary of trees circling the clearing, I stop and stare. A myriad of stones are haphazardly scattered everywhere with a larger one positioned in the middle, almost as a focal point to the group, but that's not what catches my attention. Sitting on top of the central stone is a chair carved out of rock. Moss and leaves cover the seat and the elements have darkened the stone. It's been here undisturbed for a long time.

Nervously, I approach the chair, taking care not to trip over any of the surrounding stones that are visible while also avoiding any that may be buried and hidden under the forest floor. There seems to be no reason or rhyme to the placement of the stones, except for the throne-like structure sitting on its stone plinth in the center of the clearing. On reaching the chair, I inspect it but can see no markings or indicators as to who built it or for what purpose. I do know there are many cultures who have created sacred places made of stone; however, apart from its seemingly random placement within the forest, there's nothing unusual or strange about it.

Shrugging, I brush the dead, dry leaves off the seat, take my backpack off and sit down on the chair. The stone is cold and hard against my ass through my jeans, but it's better than sitting on the ground and getting grubby. Although, I'm probably filthy anyway, having spent some time unconscious on the bed back at Gregory's mom's house. I let out a shudder, and debate whether this would be a good place to change my clothes. Glancing around, I listen hard, but can't detect any human sounds or see anyone approaching.

I decide to risk it, and standing up, I lift my backpack onto the stone seat. I quickly strip off my clothes, discarding them on the ground by my feet, and pull out a fresh t-shirt, underwear, and leggings. A rustle behind me draws my attention and jolting my head up, I spin around, looking for the source of the noise. I turn three hundred and sixty degrees, my eyes darting everywhere, checking to make sure no one is there, but I don't see anyone lurking beyond the tree line. Feeling more vulnerable than I did a moment ago, I hurriedly pull on the fresh clothes, wishing I could have showered first but relieved to be covered up once more.

As I stow away my dirty clothes into the backpack, I notice the photographs I took from. Mom's box and pick them up. I stare at the photo of Mom and me and run a finger over our smiling faces before tucking it behind the picture of the stranger. I'm still not sure why I brought this one with me. I don't know who he is, but some part of me couldn't leave it behind with the others. I feel like I've seen him before, but that's impossible because I'd remember if I'd encountered this man previously.

I've had crushes in the past, on boys at school and once even a teacher, but I've never felt the creeping blush or hot rush of curiosity and desire I feel when I look at him. It's his eyes; they seem to bore right into my soul. It's ridiculous how much I'm drawn to the man in this damn photo, but I can't seem to switch it off. No doubt this is someone my mom encountered, so I shouldn't be having these thoughts for that reason alone, because he'll be much older now than he was when this was taken.

I flip it over, suddenly wondering if she's written anything on the back. I didn't think to look before. There's nothing but a blank space on the other side, and disappointed, I turn it back over and look at him again. I feel foolish for having such a strong reaction to a photo, but I can't help it. My body heats the longer his unmoving eyes stare into mine, and I feel the same need I felt back in the coffee shop, starting to build within me. With no one around to view my shame, I tentatively slide my free hand down the front of my leggings.

I gasp in shock as the motion lowers the material and my bare skin kisses the cold stone beneath my ass. I press my fingers against the spot that's begging to be touched and slowly start to stroke the tiny bundle of nerves before pressing harder, rubbing faster, chasing the sensations that are running through my body like electricity. The eyes in the photo I'm clutching onto almost feel like they're watching me, egging me on, urging me to succumb to the pleasure. I dip my fingers into my soaking wet pussy, delving deep inside before withdrawing them. As I swirl the juices around my clit with my wet fingers, I grip the stony arm of the seat, panting in between whimpers as I approach the crest of the wave flowing through me. My eyes close as I reach the peak and tumble over, shuddering and crying out as I ride the sensations rippling through my body.

I shake through the aftershocks still racking my body as I come down from the high of pleasure. My breathing slows and my heartbeat starts to regulate. I straighten myself out and look thoughtfully down at the photo I'm still holding in my lap. That was intense, more so than any of the previous orgasms

I've ever succeeded in giving myself, and I'm sure his image was the cause. Shaking my head, I tuck the photo away in my backpack and finally pull out the envelope I stole from the chest of drawers at Gregory's mom's house.

Nervousness makes my hand shake as I stare at the name written on the front, and I flip it over, lifting the flap at the back to open it. My heart is stuttering in my chest again, and I'm almost afraid of what I'm going to learn about my family. I've no idea what this envelope contains, and a small part of me doesn't want to know. Gregory was right about one thing, though: the not knowing is eating me up inside. Mom never wanted me to know anything about my daddy, but now I do, it's lit a burning need inside me, prompting me to find out more. I'm hoping that the contents will answer some, if not all, of the questions I've been asking myself and my mom ever since I was a little girl.

Chapter Eight

I open the envelope, and I'm disappointed to see there are only photographs inside. I was hoping for some kind of letter, or anything that might give me more details about my history. Carefully, I remove them, and place the envelope on my lap with the photos on top. I pick up the first one and smile; it's a photo of Mom holding me when I was a newborn baby. She looks so young.

I turn it over and see unfamiliar handwriting on the back, and the words, 'Kayley and Sofia'. Setting it aside, I pick up the next one and my stomach jolts unpleasantly when I see my mom and Gregory staring back up at me. I flick through the rest and see more photos of me and Mom, and her and Gregory. Finally, one catches my eye. It's a family photo. I can see Gregory, his batshit crazy mom, and a lot of other people including the fascinating stranger...the man I don't recognize but feel so strongly drawn to. I flip it over and see 'Greene Family' is written on the back.

As I begin to replace the photos in the envelope, I notice one more, smaller than the others, and I lift it up to take a closer look. It's of Mom, and she's standing next to the stranger. I stare down at the picture; confirmation that he's a part of her past is right there in front of my eyes, and his hand is wrapped possessively over her stomach. With shaking hands, I turn the photo over and read the words, 'Kayley Richards and Luke Greene are having a baby. Kayley is 8 weeks pregnant'. I drop it into my lap and cover my mouth with my hands. 'Greene'...*fucking hell!*

I shove the rest of the photos back inside the envelope, then sliding off the chair, I hastily return them to my backpack. I push them to the bottom as if I'm hoping to bury them and pretend I didn't do what I just did...I fucked myself to orgasm with my hand while staring at the picture of a man I thought was a stranger, only to discover that's far from the truth. *This is so messed up!* The thought he might be my real daddy turns my stomach, but I can't seem to erase from my mind all the desire and mystery that surrounds him, not while the juices of my release still remain slick on my pussy.

A crack of a twig draws my attention, and I snap my eyes up in the direction the noise came from in time to see a man enter the clearing. Quickly, I turn and finish packing all my stuff into my backpack. Thank goodness, he didn't come sooner, or he'd have seen me with my leggings and panties pulled down, sitting on a cold stone chair in the middle of the woods, hand between my thighs in the throes of pleasure, rubbing one out to a photo of a man who may be my daddy. *Fucking awkward!*

"Who the hell are you? What the fuck are you doing on my property?" a gruff voice makes me jump, and I turn back around to face him.

"I, um…" I trail off, staring open mouthed.

My backpack slips from my slack hand and drops to the floor with a thud. I must be dreaming because there's no way…*he* can't be real.

"I won't ask you again. Now, answer the question," he snaps impatiently, but I still don't respond, I'm too stunned.

Years have passed, but there's no mistaking the dark, piercing eyes staring at me from across the clearing, emanating angry curiosity. He's older, but it's only made him look even more rugged and handsome than before. I curse myself for thinking it, but it's the truth.

"S-Sofia," I stammer, tripping over my words as I rush to answer him.

I want to ask him about my mom, about everything, but I'm too shocked to speak. Shame makes my cheeks redden when I think about what I did and how he'd react if he knew. I jump down from the stone plinth on which the chair sits, and his dark eyes track my movements. I'm embarrassed to feel the wetness in my panties increase the longer his gaze remains on me, and I feel sick to my stomach.

"Sorry for trespassing," I mumble, as I stand upright and move to walk past him, not realizing in my foolish daze he's already closed some of the distance between us.

"You didn't answer my question, little girl," he says, clamping a firm hand around my upper arm and halting me.

I attempt to tug my arm away, but his hand tightens as he waits for me to explain myself. My heart is pounding and my legs are shaking. I'm face to face with the man who might be my daddy, and I'm too scared to say anything.

"I'm looking for my real daddy. My mom died and my stepdad is an alcoholic and an asshole," I finally confess to him in a small voice.

I look down at my feet to avoid his gaze, but I can still feel his eyes on me. I fight the urge to squirm, and tamp down the sickness that's threatening to follow. Gregory's face flashes into my mind, and I shudder.

"That doesn't explain why you're here, on my property, and sitting in that chair without my permission," he growls, and I cry out as his hand pinches tighter.

I look directly up at him, staring him dead in the face, unable to keep my eyes averted. So many years have passed. Has he forgotten about my mom? Gregory said she'd lied about miscarrying me, so I guess there's no reason he'd try to see himself or my mom in me. I will him to notice the resemblance, to see something in my face, my eyes, or anything that might reveal my identity. I don't want to be the one to have to mention it.

"Leave and don't come back, little girl. You're not welcome here," he finally says, shoving me away.

I stumble and trip over my feet, trying not to lose my balance.

"No," I whisper as he turns and walks away, disappearing through the trees.

I scramble to my feet and run after him. Hearing my pursuit, he turns around to look at me. The expression on his face is terrifying, and I quail beneath the weight of it being directed toward me.

"My name is Sofia," I repeat in a weak voice.

He snorts, crossing his arms over his broad chest.

"You already said that. Now, beat it, little girl."

"Sofia Greene," I repeat, and even though his expression remains unchanged, something flickers in his eyes…recognition maybe?

"Who sent you here?" he questions in a low and deadly tone full of threat.

"N-no one. I found papers in my mom's closet and then an envelope of photos in my stepdad's crazy momma's house. I wasn't sent by anyone. I ran away and found this place by accident," I blurt out, gesturing at the clearing and taking a step back; for the first time, I'm afraid to be in his presence.

Mom didn't want me to know anything about my daddy, and if this man really is my daddy, then I've really fucked up. Not just because of my visceral reaction to the photo, but because I'm beginning to understand why she feared me finding out the truth.

Chapter Nine

"Prove it," he says, looking down at me with a penetrative stare.

"Right now?" I ask as I glance around us.

He raises an eyebrow. "Did I say later?"

I squirm under the intensity of his gaze and look down as I swing my backpack off my shoulder and open it. Rummaging through, I pull out the envelope of photographs, the papers containing details of my birth and legal name change, and the photographs I took from Mom's box. Silently, still looking down at my feet, I hold them out for him to take, but he doesn't; instead, he just continues to stare at me. I feel self-conscious, standing there like an idiot holding out this stuff to him.

I don't know what he's waiting for. I flick through the photos to find the one of him and my mom and show it to him, but he gives it no more than a passing glance. Finally, lifting my eyes to meet his, we stare wordlessly at each other. He seems to be searching for something, but what, I don't know. The scrutinizing way he's eyeing me makes my body erupt in chills, and I want to shiver. I'm not sure what it is about him, but I'm curious and afraid in equal measures. An illicit yearning has burrowed deep inside me. It's in my blood, and it sickens me that I still feel it, even after my unexpected enlightenment barely ten minutes ago.

His eyes are dark, but I can see the golden-brown tones hiding in the shadows, and I realize why my mom told me I had my daddy's eyes. It's like looking into a reflection, but if the eyes are the windows to the soul, then there's nothing but darkness lurking within his. I'm breathless; fear, elation, and something deeper runs through me, but I can't pinpoint why my reaction to him is so visceral.

As he continues to study me, I feel the same telltale butterflies fluttering in my stomach that I get when staring at his photograph. He's much older than he was in that image, but somehow he's even more handsome now with the gray flecks in his hair and in the scruff on his chin. My body reacts, unbidden, and something must show in my face because I see the barest hint of a reaction in his eyes. His expression changes, but instead of anger or whatever the hell emotion he should be expressing, he smirks with amusement.

He rubs his chin thoughtfully.

"Come along then," he says, finally.

I blink stupidly up at him, surprised by the sudden change in his tone from unwelcoming to inviting. Without waiting for me to respond, he turns to walk away while I remain standing there, not moving.

"Don't make me repeat myself. You won't like it if I do," he throws over his shoulder, not even bothering to look, somehow knowing I'm still in the same place I was a moment ago.

I quickly tuck the handful of papers and photos into my backpack and hurry after him, running to catch up and match his long strides. I'm trying not to trip over any stones and tree roots lurking beneath the fallen leaves, but it's hard to focus when I'm walking beside the one man I've spent most of my life yearning to know.

I stumble and fall onto my knees, and feel the skin split beneath the material of my leggings, but I push aside the pain, and scrambling to my feet, I hurry to catch up again. We've not been walking for long when we reach a large stone house; it's the one from Mom's photo with the same truck out front looking older but still in good condition. There's something cold about the building, but after living with Gregory for so many years, I'd much rather take coldness over heated, drunken rages.

I'll never go back to Mom's house. There's

nothing left for me there, except an empty hole in my heart where she used to live and memories tarnished with hatred. This is the fate I chose for myself when I abandoned everything in pursuit of a long-faded but never forgotten dream. I wanted to know where I came from and the identity of my real daddy, and now I'm here and he's in front of my eyes. He's real and so much more intriguing than I'd ever dared to hope.

I follow him into the house, looking behind me one last time at the trees and the narrow, trodden down path we walked along to get here. I frown, realizing I never asked him why the stone chair was there and what was so special about it. Mentally shrugging, I set aside the questions for later and take in my surroundings as he leads me along a hallway and into a large family room.

He drops down onto a couch and stretches out his legs, nodding at the empty seat next to him. Nervously, I walk across the room and sit down beside him. I'm on edge, not knowing what to do or say. Eighteen years is a long time. He may be my daddy, but I don't know anything else about him; he's a complete stranger to me. *How can we begin to bridge the gap between us?*

Chapter Ten

The silence drags on awkwardly, and a part of me is terrified to shatter it. I know nothing about my daddy beyond the few mentions of him my mom made when I pressured her for information, and the scathing remarks made by both Gregory and his crazy momma whom, I now realize, are more connected to me than I knew or would like. I want to speak, but I'm not sure what to say. It was one thing to dream of this moment, but another entirely to be experiencing it.

My head is spinning, my heart is racing, my breaths are coming in short, sharp pants, and my hands are balled into clammy fists on my lap.

"You need to relax. You'll give yourself an aneurysm if you stay all tensed up like that," he says, and when I jump at the sound of his voice, he chuckles.

I laugh nervously and attempt to loosen up my muscles and do as he says. His tone may have been friendly, but there's no mistaking the instruction in his words. He's perfectly at ease with his long legs stretched out, and his arms spread out across the back of the couch. I feel small compared to him, and it's not just in height and build. His presence is all encompassing, filling the room with the essence of him.

Finally relaxing, somewhat, I dig deep for the courage I felt when I ran from Gregory and took control of my fate. Summoning it to the surface, I look toward my daddy and gulp down the fear I'm feeling. Mentally, I shrug off all preconceived notions I have from the dark picture Mom painted of him and slide up the couch closer to him. I want to know more, and the curiosity I've buried within me for so long finally starts to resurface. The flood-gates to my mouth open, and the questions start pouring out.

"So, how long have you lived here? How old are you? How did you meet my mom? What should I call you? Have you got any other kids?" I rattle off.

I haven't seen anyone else here, but that doesn't mean there's no one. I could have siblings I don't know about.

"You've not been here long, so I'll forgive you this once because you don't know the rules yet. Don't ask questions. My business is not your business, and just because you're family, it doesn't mean you're entitled to know shit. Yes, I have other kids. No I'm not going to talk about them. You'll meet them soon enough, I expect. You can call me Pater, like the others do," he tells me, and I'm taken aback by his blunt response.

"Rules?" I question tentatively, trying to make it sound more like a statement than a question, but failing while kicking myself for letting him make me feel belittled already.

His eyes darken, and his lips twitch before spreading into a smile.

"There aren't many, and they're not hard to learn. Don't ask questions, don't go upstairs without permission, and don't ever lie to me. I'll always know when you disobey me, and you won't enjoy the consequences if you break the rules. There are others, but you'll pick them up as you go along," he responds, and the clear threat makes my heart jolt.

I sit silently, staring at him, unsure what I should say or do. He stares back at me, his smile and darkened eyes alighting on mine. Slowly, he drags his gaze over my face and down my body. I shift uncomfortably, still aware of how close he came to catching me back in that clearing, pleasuring myself to his photo, only to discover, shortly after, the moral implications of what I'd done. A part of me wonders if he saw me before he approached, but I'm fairly certain my actions went unseen. Honestly,

I have no idea what he'd have thought, and I'm not sure I want to find out.

I know I shouldn't, but a small part of me envisions him spanking me for my transgressions, and it takes everything in me not to squirm at the thought of his large hands chastising my body. I mentally shake my head to clear it and smile faintly at him, forcing some kind of acknowledgement of his words. My skin prickles with awareness, and I turn to meet a set of eyes peering through the doorway. I blink and they're gone; it was so quick I may have imagined them.

My stomach rumbles, and I follow Pater's eyes as he glances at a clock on the mantle. I'm surprised to see that it's so late. He stands up and stretches, and I peek as subtly as I can at the abs beneath his shirt when it lifts with his movements. *What the hell is wrong with me?* I shouldn't be acting like this, let alone entertaining any of these thoughts I'm having. He's my daddy, my blood, my family. It's wrong, it's disgusting, and I'm ashamed of myself for thinking them at all.

He looks at me and then turns to leave the room.

"Come on. Dinner will be ready in a moment."

I hurriedly get to my feet and follow after him through the door and along a narrow hallway into a large kitchen. In the center is a wooden dining table with six matching chairs surrounding it. He takes a seat at the head of the table and gestures for me to sit in the chair adjacent to him. Nervousness prickles through me, and I have to stifle a gasp when I see a young man, who can't be much younger in age than me, standing by the counter staring sullenly at us.

He's slim with dark hair, and his sharp angular features closely resemble Pater's. In an instant, I know this is one of his other children.

"Vaughn, stop staring and bring the food over," our daddy barks at him, and I jump in surprise at the harsh tone.

A warning look from Vaughn when I open my mouth to speak shuts me up, and I sit in silence while he obeys the instruction. Soon the plates are on the table and the smell and sight of the food makes my mouth water. Another young boy walks into the room, and after glancing shyly at me, he takes a seat. I notice that the plates in front of us hold a much simpler and smaller portion of food than Pater's, but I'm too hungry to question it. Vaughn sits opposite me, and the remaining chair remains empty. I pick up my fork and prepare to dig in, but a sharp kick on my ankle under the table makes me gasp, and I glare at Vaughn. *What gives him the right to boss me around and kick me? He doesn't even know me.*

Pater picks up his fork and takes a bite of the food and then glances between me and his son.

"Kid, behave around your sister. Don't want to

end up like Jocelyn, do you? Speaking of, have you visited her today?" he asks, his tone taking on a stern edge, and I watch as Vaughn's face pales before he shakes his head and drops his gaze to his plate.

My stomach is in knots. I'm not sure what to make of all of this, but I keep my thoughts to myself. I concentrate on my food until it's gone, and I stay put when our daddy stands up and exits the kitchen, leaving me alone with my siblings.

Chapter Eleven

Over the next few days, I settle into an uneasy routine. I'm still learning the rules and getting to know the family. I've met Vaughn and the youngest boy who I've since learned is called Eloy, but I have yet to meet Jocelyn. I've asked Vaughn about her a few times, but he refuses to answer any questions about the family. Eloy is quiet and doesn't really speak much around me, or engage in conversation, so I can't ask him, and I'm not sure I'm willing to risk upsetting our daddy by asking him and breaking one of his cardinal rules. He said I'd meet his other kids soon enough, but Jocelyn is still a mystery to me.

I'm slowly beginning to find my place, in the house at least, but I've still yet to discover what my role and position will be as a part of this family. I want nothing to do with Gregory and his mom in spite of the fact we're related. As far as I'm concerned, my daddy and my half-siblings are all I've got left in this world.

The house is so quiet most of the time, and I often catch myself treading lightly like I'm stepping on eggshells, trying not to break them. I've put the reason I'm feeling unsettled by the silence down to the stark contrast between where I am now and where I come from. Occasionally, however, the tension is almost palpable, particularly when I'm around Vaughn and Pater and the questions are burning inside me. Eloy is fearful when our father is in the room and quietly behaves, but I've noticed how Vaughn looks out for him and me. I'm desperate to unravel the mystery of Jocelyn, and I'm still trying to find my feet and not shoulder any of the weight of whatever is at play in this house. I've found myself often wondering, while lying in my bed at night, what I've gotten myself into. One thing's for sure, it's better than what I've left behind me…so far, at least.

It's late, really late, at night during my second week here when the sounds of sex reach my ears. Heavy grunts that can only belong to Pater filter through the floorboards, and the high keen of a female blends in erotically. I shift and roll over, attempting to ignore them, and the effect they're having on me. *I shouldn't be thinking these thoughts. I shouldn't be having these thoughts.* I repeat the words over and over in my head, willing my body and mind to obey. I do my best to ignore the way my nipples harden at the sounds of the woman he's pleasuring and disregard the tangible wetness between my thighs at the thought of what he's doing to her to elicit such a response.

I close my eyes tightly, and squeeze my legs together, hating the ache that's burning down there, begging to be released. Unable to curb the cravings, which first began with the photograph of a stranger, I cave into them and slide my hand downward, moaning softly at the contact of my fingers against my clit and slick folds. I'm so wet, and it's so wrong, but the forbidden is taunting me into sin and darkness, and I want to indulge in an oblivion of pleasure.

I cry out when I'm getting close, and I barely manage to stifle the sound that threatens to escape by biting my lip with my teeth. I'm too far gone to stop when I hear my bedroom door opening and then closing, I'm lost in the delirium of sensation flooding through my system. Another cry almost escapes as the orgasm crests through me, and a hand clamps down over my mouth, trapping it inside. Tremors of pleasure ripple through me as I stare into a pair of startlingly familiar brown eyes. There's a wariness in them, shielding secrets I want to know, but they lack the soullessness that lingers in Pater's...they belong to Vaughn.

The sounds upstairs subside, and I'm trapped in a maelstrom of confusion and shame as my body calms and my heart rate slows. Vaughn holds his hand where it is while soft footsteps on the floor above and then on the stairs reach our ears before fading away to nothing. He removes his hand from my mouth, and we both stare at each other.

Awkwardness starts to sink in at the thought of being caught by my brother getting off to the sound of our daddy fucking someone in the rooms above us. I remove my hand from between my legs and look away. The thin curtain hanging over the window does nothing to filter out the moonlight, and it's just clear enough to see his pale face.

He lifts his hand from my mouth and slowly backs away from me. I'm frozen in place, still stunned from his sudden presence and being caught touching myself. Without saying a word, he leaves the room, quietly shutting the door behind him, and moments later I hear heavy footsteps on the stairs before the house falls deathly quiet once again. No sound disturbs the silence, not even a creak of the house or whisper of wind past my window. It's strange, especially with the forest on our doorstep. Deciding I'm imagining things, I curl up beneath the blanket and close my eyes, letting myself drift off into an uneasy, dreamless sleep.

Chapter Twelve

Vaughn's daily, morning wake up knock on my bedroom door rouses me from a light slumber, and I stare up at the ceiling while my body slowly catches up with my mind. The room I've been given is plain, bland almost, with white walls and a simple bed with white sheets and a woolen blanket.

Sitting up, I shove the curtains open and lean forward to grab my backpack that's slung over the post at the end of my bed. I still haven't unpacked everything, and I try not to dwell on why that is. I tip it upside down, allowing the contents to spill onto the blanket. I haven't looked at any of this stuff since I came here, but I want to now. Ignoring the papers with the details of my birth and name change, I reach for the envelope and loose photos scattered in front of me.

I leaf through them, looking for the photo of

my mom and me. Finding it, I hold it up to the light and take in the similarities between us. She looks happy in this picture, and it hurts that I don't remember this moment we spent together. Too many bad recollections of living with her and Gregory and having him trail along on our days out have scrubbed many of the happier memories clean from my mind.

The other photo I've been trying to forget about sits on the bed. His dark brown eyes affect me like they've done every time before, but the image does nothing to convey the power of that stare when it's being leveled directly at me, up close and very real. My head aches with the conflict inside it as I desperately try to cope with the wrongness of my response to him and force myself to morph my feelings into something more appropriate for a daughter. Familial love is one thing, but this is beyond the norm of anything I should be experiencing. The deep carnal desire wars with my morality, and it scares me to know how much I want to give in to it.

I should leave here, run far, far away, and never look back. There's nothing else for me out there, though. Everything I want and need is here, but I'm not certain how permanent this arrangement is going to be. I want to stay, even though fear of my emotions makes my soul restless. Memories of the previous night start to trickle to the forefront of my mind, making my stomach warm, and a familiar ache pulses between my legs.

I shove the photos back into my bag, and before I can slip into a daydream, I swing my legs out of bed. Stripping off my sleep shirt, I let it fall to the floor and grab fresh clothes from the chest of drawers, the only other item of furniture in the room. I'm just about to pull on my bra when the sound of my bedroom door bursting open makes me jump. I let out a squeal and drop my bra in surprise as I whip around to see my daddy standing in the doorway.

"Laziness will not be tolerated in this house. You should already be dressed and at the dining table with your breakfast by now. I've been damned patient, letting you settle and find your place, but you're a part of this family, and you can't just rely on the others to get shit done. You've got to pull your weight too, girl," he growls, moving toward me, eyes raking over my disheveled appearance and exposed body.

I frantically try to cover myself up with my hands, and grabbing my t-shirt from the bed, I pull it over my head, one-handed. His eyes burn into me, and I feel incredibly small when he stands in front of me, close enough to touch, towering over me with a frown on his handsome features. His proximity and the annoyance rolling off him in waves makes me momentarily forget what I'm doing.

"Get dressed, and get your ass into that kitchen," he orders in a low tone.

I stare up at him, dumbstruck. I've never been spoken to like that before. I understand sharing the chores, but Mom never ruled our house like this, and Gregory was too busy pissing away all our money on alcohol to care that much.

"Get a move on, or you can go out there as you are with my handprint glowing on that pale ass of yours. Doesn't matter much to me either way, but I suggest you decide quickly," he threatens, still watching me.

I jump into action, pulling on my panties and leggings, very aware of his eyes tracking my every movement. Self-consciousness makes my cheeks hot, and I do everything I can to avoid his gaze while I finish getting dressed. I quickly move past him in my hurry to get out of the room, but his hand on my shoulder stops me dead.

"Good girl, next time you won't disappoint me, will you?" he asks, but it's more of a statement than a question.

"No," I reply quietly.

"I didn't quite catch that, Sofia," he says, still holding me in place.

"No, Pater," I repeat, and he lets me go with a chuckle.

"That wasn't so hard, was it? Now, get a move on."

My heart is beating fast, and my head is spinning as I try to make sense of what happened and clear my mind of the fog his presence creates. He's everywhere, even when he's not, and it makes it hard to breathe. In some ways, after so many years without him, it's comforting to have such a tangible presence of him around, but it's also hard to suppress the unnerving feeling it creates in me.

I make it to the kitchen in time to finish laying the table with Vaughn. I'm tempted to ask him why he didn't come in and ask me to help when he knocked earlier; however, after his unexpected and awkward visit last night, combined with the tension I'm still experiencing from the interaction with my daddy, I decide to hold my tongue for once. *Curiosity can go fuck itself for now, or at least until I've managed to calm my racing heart and clear my head a little.*

Breakfast is quiet with nothing audible apart from the sounds of eating and drinking, but I can't relax. My whole body is wound tight as a bowstring, and I feel like I'm about to snap. I'm picking at my food, and Vaughn's eyes are boring into me with a mixture of curiosity and something else. I can easily ignore his stare, but my daddy's eyes haven't once left me either, and the slightly narrowed, thoughtful look paired with a somewhat playful smirk has my stomach twisting with unease. Eloy seems happily oblivious to the added tension between me and

Pater, or he's just too focused on the meal to pay attention.

I'm not sure how to feel about any of this, and the longer I stay in this house the more confused I'm becoming. By time the plates are empty and I've helped Vaughn wash them I feel like screaming. Usually Pater leaves the table and goes upstairs or to the family room, but this morning, he stays put, watching us as we go about our after breakfast chores.

"Sofia, come to the family room when you're done," he says finally, and leaves the room.

"What do you think he wants?" I ask Vaughn nervously, as we hurry to finish putting away the plates.

Vaughn shrugs and shakes his head, eyeing the space where our daddy was just sitting.

"Don't keep him waiting," is all he says before lapsing into silence again.

Once all the chores are complete, Vaughn leaves through the back door, and I desperately want to follow him outside instead of facing our daddy. I know I've nothing to be nervous about, but I can't stop my hands from shaking, because after last night and this morning, it's clear there's something disturbing about this place, and I've been closing my eyes to it all.

Chapter Thirteen

"Sofia, come sit down," Pater invites me to sit beside him on the couch, but I can hear the undertone that tells me not to fuck around.

I've already delayed as long as I can, lingering in the kitchen and making sure everything was clean. When Vaughn returned from outside and saw me still in there, he'd shaken his head at me in dismay before pointing at the hallway leading to the family room. He didn't utter a word, but he didn't need to. I knew what he wasn't saying; I'm going to be in trouble because I kept our daddy waiting.

Gingerly, I take a seat, waiting for Pater to blow up or lash out like I'm used to experiencing with Gregory. He doesn't speak for a while, and my whole body is screaming at me because it feels like I've not taken a breath since I walked in here. He quirks an eyebrow at my hesitancy, and I force myself to sink lower into the seat.

For some reason, I always feel incredibly on edge when we're alone in a room together. I'm not sure why that is; whether it's how we met, the sick and twisted desires I've been having...or it's simply just him. Maybe it's a combination of all three. I'm not certain what he wants from me right now, but I do know he's probably going to punish me for making him wait and ignoring a direct instruction.

"This morning," he begins.

I cut him off. "I'm sorry! I promise it won't happen again. I overslept, and then I got distracted looking at photos of my mom. I'm still adjusting, I guess. I didn't realize I needed to help with breakfast."

His jaw tightens, and his eyes flash, and I realize too late what I've done. I've interrupted him when he was speaking. I recognize the expression, a precursor to one of Gregory's outbursts. I hold my breath until my chest feels tight, waiting for him to blow his top and lose control, but it doesn't happen.

"Don't you dare interrupt me when I'm speaking, Sofia. I don't take kindly to rudeness from anyone, especially not from my kids," he warns, and his menacing tone is more frightening than if he'd yelled the words at me.

"I'm sorry..." I start again.

"Keep your mouth closed, girl. Or I'll shut you

up for talking back to me when *I am speaking*." He enunciates his last words with a shout, and I jump, scooting along the couch as far away from him as possible without getting up.

I want so badly to run, but instinct and the look in his eyes tell me to fucking stay put, or I'll only make things worse for myself.

"Here I was, thinking it was about time I got to know my daughter, and here *you* are, giving me cheek and making me nearly lose my damn patience. If that had been one of my other kids, I'd have lost my temper by now. They know exactly what will happen to them if they disrespect me. I think I've been very generous, don't you? So don't push your luck any more than you have already, Sofia," he finishes, his tone much calmer.

"Sorry, Pater," I say quietly, and he nods his head in approval.

He gestures for me to come closer, and I oblige, too scared to do anything that might make him shout again.

"How did you find me here?" he asks, and I stare up at him, biting my lip, surprised at the unexpected change in direction of the conversation.

"My mom hid who you were from me when she was alive. She wouldn't tell me your name or anything about you. After she died, I didn't want to stay with my stepdad; it was horrible there with just him, not that it was much better before. When I searched through a box of mom's things, I discovered some old photographs and all my birth documents. I didn't know it was you in one of the images I found until later. I ran away and went in search of the house listed on my birth certificate. That's where I met my stepdad's crazy momma. She and my stepdad drugged me and tied me up. I managed to get away, but it was there I found the envelope with the family photos. How I found you, though, was a complete accident. After I escaped, I was walking in the forest and came across the clearing with the stone chair. That's when I discovered who you were, and you arrived soon after."

I finish telling him, glossing over the part where Gregory tried to rape me at his momma's house.

"What were you doing in the clearing, Sofia? You didn't look like you were there by accident. You were sitting on that chair like it was *made* for you," Pater questions, and I swallow down the small gasp threatening to burst from my chest. *Does he know?*

"Nothing, I stopped to rest. I was tired and hadn't eaten in a while. I was scared that Gregory and his mom would find me, and I was hiding from them," I blurt out, but I can feel the heat rising in my cheeks as flashes of what I was doing, while staring at my daddy's photo, pop into my mind.

"Really?" he says in a disbelieving tone, and my eyes widen as I stare at him, "Because I don't think you're telling me the whole truth, Sofia. Now, why would that be?"

"I'm not lying," I assure him, but of course, he's right.

I'm not telling him the whole truth, and somehow, he seems to know that. Maybe he can tell I'm not divulging everything, or maybe he did see me that day after all. I don't want to tell him. It's embarrassing and wrong, and he will be disgusted by me. I need this place, I need my family, even if they're still strangers to me. If he knows the truth, he'll throw me out on my ass like a disgusting piece of trash. I've only just found them, and if I'm forced to leave I've nowhere else to go but Mom's, and I don't want to go back there.

I'm thrown back to my first evening here when I was sitting in this exact same spot with Pater's eyes boring holes into my soul, seemingly scooping out my light to replace it with his darkness. I don't want to tell him what I did, and I'll take whatever punishment he decides to give me rather than admit it to him.

"There you go again, telling more lies. You're only making it worse for yourself. I told you, Sofia, I always know. I'll ask you one last time; what were you doing in that chair? I want to hear the words, and I want the truth this time. Think you can do that?"

I suck in a breath before mumbling, "I'm not lying."

"*Bull shit*." he splits the word for emphasis. "My other kids know not to lie to me, not that it stops them from trying. I know about everything that goes on under my roof, and secrets don't stay secret for long."

Chapter Fourteen

He knows about everything that goes on under his roof? Does that mean he knows what I was doing the last night when Vaughn walked into my room? My cheeks heat, and I can't do a thing to stop the blush from coloring them. He may not know what I did last night, but I'm almost certain he saw more than I ever would have wanted him to witness on the day we first met. *How long was he watching me? What must he think of me, now he knows he's my daddy?*

"Get back over here, Sofia. I'm not done with you, yet," he says, scowling at me, and I realize I'm perched at the very end of the couch, ready to flee the room if he loses his temper.

Reluctantly, I move up the couch until I'm sitting next to him again, and the heat from his body so close to mine heats my chilled skin, fear having sapped the warmth from me.

"Now, you're going to sit here and tell me what really happened that day in the clearing. I know what I saw, and I want to know if you have the guts to tell me the truth," he says, rubbing his chin as a steely glint flashes in his eyes.

I gulp and fidget in my seat, uncomfortably aware of what he's asking me to reveal. I've been trying to avoid this, but the longer I draw out the silence, the more unforgiving his expression is becoming. I know full well that I'm encouraging the darkness within him to rise to the surface, not that I believe it has far to travel; it's always there, lingering, with malice at its heart and a fire in its belly.

Stay and obey, or fight and flee? My body hums with the need to get away from him. However, I suspect if I try, it won't end well for me. His body is relaxed, but I can see an awareness of my inner turmoil in his gaze and in the way his lips are turned up at the corners as he scrutinizes me. *Is he able to read what's flowing through my mind right now?* I gulp, and my chest rises and falls rapidly with fast, shallow breaths. I'm fighting back a terrible mix of fear and desire, and I don't know how to calm my racing heart.

Instinct takes over and I leap up, heading for the door, but I barely make it out of my seat before a large hand grabs mine and yanks me backward into the steel cage of his arms. I'm now a hostage not only to him but to the illicit desires flowing through my veins, warping my heart and cursing me for my damning thoughts and inner cravings.

"I didn't give you permission to leave my presence," Pater whispers in my ear, his hot breath blowing over my face and making me shiver.

His voice is calm, pleasant even, but I sense that years of controlling every aspect of his and his children's lives has helped him perfect that smooth tone, even when he's anything but calm. The menace behind his words reveals the anger beneath his cool exterior, and I know I've really fucked up.

"You've had your chance. Now, I'll tell you what I saw. I saw a dirty little girl fucking herself with her hand like it was a thick hard cock while sitting on a chair that was built by *my* hand for my wife and the mother of my children. *Then,* after I'd already caught you trespassing you came prancing up to me, a perfect picture of innocence and sweetness, and told me that you're my kid," he says, holding me tightly against himself while I squirm and struggle to get free.

My frightened whimpers are smothered beneath the volume of his voice that's laced heavily with sarcasm. "Tell me, am I wrong, Sofia?" he dares me, and I twist around to look into his eyes, heart pounding so loudly he must hear it.

"You're not wrong, Pater," I mumble, and he raises his eyebrows and smirks.

"Well, damn. Did my ears deceive me, or did

you just 'fess up?" he exclaims, leaning back to look at me, his golden-brown eyes gleaming.

I bite my lip nervously, and he chuckles.

"You've got more balls than most of my kids, Sofia. That doesn't mean you're getting off easy, though. You lied and disobeyed me, and I know there's more to this little story than you've admitted. You need to decide if I'm going to have to tell the rest, or if you're going to continue this little ballsy streak you've got going and reveal all. What's it going to be?"

He levels me with his soul-piercing gaze, and I close my eyes, foolishly trying to hide from it, but there's no hiding from Pater. He's made it clear he sees and knows everything, and I'm not sure how well I can keep my secrets buried when he's here digging them up, uncovering them with his words.

"The photo...I was looking at a photo I took from my mom's box. It was the..." I take a deep breath, trembling as I recall what happened, trying to build up the courage to say the words out loud, "...the photo of you."

I cower down, trying to make myself as small as the arms banded around me will allow, but Pater doesn't let me shrink away from the dreadful repercussions of my own admission; instead, he maneuvers my body onto his lap and forces me to face him.

"Good girl! I can tell that was hard to admit, but

see how much better it feels to tell the truth. Now, there's still that little issue of trying to hide shit and avoid me that we need to deal with. I'm not happy, and just because you're new around here doesn't mean I'm going to go easy on you. My kids are expected to follow the rules, and they reap the consequences when they misbehave. Your momma tried to keep you from me, but you're a part of this family, and it's time you learned what that really means," Pater says, running a hand down my arm.

My gaze flies up to meet his, and the darkness emanating from his eyes sends a chill down my spine. His grip on me tightens. I'm pulled more firmly against his hard chest and something else that steals my breath.

"Are-are you hard right now?" I ask in astonishment, eyes wide and searching.

"Why do you sound so surprised, considering it was you who made yourself come while thinking about me? Don't pretend this isn't what you've wanted all along. You pictured it, fucked yourself to the thought of my thick, hard cock ramming into you and stealing that precious virginity of yours."

"No. I don't want that," I blurt out, leaning away from him, heart pounding and staring at him in shocked disbelief.

"You know what I think, Sofia. I think you're a little liar who's trying to get herself in trouble because she wants to be punished. So far almost every word that has come out of your mouth has been to defy me," he retorts, grinding himself against me.

I close my eyes, ashamed of how I'm feeling and the way my body responds, unbidden, to the friction and his proximity.

"I'm not a liar, and I'm not trying to get into trouble with you, Pater," I continue in denial, afraid to face the truth.

Pater pushes me from his lap, and I fall unceremoniously to the floor. I sit there stunned for a moment until I see him lean toward me, and the instinct to flee kicks in. Seizing the chance at freedom, I scramble away from him, but his hands close around each of my ankles, and he drags me back toward him. I'm flipped over onto my back, my leggings are ripped down my legs, and he pushes two large fingers inside my pussy before I can react to what's happening.

I let out an involuntarily moan as they slide in with ease. Pater continues to fuck me with his fingers until I'm panting, and the sounds of my moans and my wetness combined are thick in the air around us. I don't even move to stop him when he frees his cock from his pants and repositions himself between my legs. One quick, brutal thrust later his cock tears into my pussy as Pater shreds my virginity, and my scream rends the air.

"Pure, just like I thought. Good girl," he praises, starting to fuck me with vigor.

The grip he has with his hands on my hips is bruising, but my body surrenders unwillingly to his touch, opening up and becoming slicker with my juices as he pounds into me, furiously. I'm crying as the mix of pain and pleasure burns me with his movements, and I'm trying frantically not to lose myself in it but failing. Eventually, he flips me onto my front and continues taking me from behind. Wrapping his hand around my long hair to form a makeshift ponytail, he uses it to hold me steady to match his rhythm. It feels as though he's tearing the strands from their roots in the vice-like grip he's fisting it with.

I shouldn't want this. I shouldn't be enjoying this. The carnal and illicit mix of pain, desire, and immorality sets alight the embers of a dark lust within my heart. He doesn't care about my pleasure, yet I feel it building anyway with every punishing thrust of his cock delving deep inside my pussy until he grunts out his release.

Without ceremony or care, he pulls out, and the blood of my virginity mixed with his cum seeps out of the hole he just invaded with his cock. Leaving me lying sprawled on the floor, he gets to his feet, and running a hand through his hair, he continues his accusations and threats as though he didn't nearly fuck the life out of me in the family room.

"Don't ever lie to me again, Sofia. I will always know. Your whore mother hid you from me and kept you ignorant about the true meaning of family. Disobedience will be punished, and lessons must be taught. I'm going to fill your cunt with seed until a child grows within your womb and you finally understand your place in our family. I will breed the familial love into your body, and you *will* accept me," he lectures me as I lie slumped at his feet.

My body is heavy, and I'm breathless as I gaze blearily up at him. I feel so foolish for not listening to my mom, but even as I stare up into his cold, dark eyes with fear growing in my soul, I know within my heart I'd still choose to be here. I came looking for my family and found it. Their blood is my blood, and at the center of it all is Pater.

"Yes, Pater," I murmur quietly, forcing myself to move.

The wide smirk that crosses his face sends a shiver rattling through me.

"Clean me," he drawls, almost lazily, as he sits down again, and reclining with his arms spread out across the back of the couch, he gestures with nothing more than a nod of his head.

His meaning is clear, and I blanch, staring at the thick cock that's still somehow hard and glistening with my blood and the juices from our fuck. His expression darkens the longer I hesitate, and I know my body won't take much more of his punishment today. I crawl over to him, settling between his legs. Drawing in a breath, I bend over, and taking his large cock in my mouth as best I can, I obey his command. I'll be a dutiful daughter and behave as my daddy tells me.

I can tell that the longer I'm kneeling there, clumsily licking, sucking, and lapping at him, the more he's losing his patience. Eventually, he grabs hold of my head, and forcing me to wrap my mouth firmly around his cock, he proceeds to fuck my throat with it. Even as I choke around his massive length, I feel myself grow wet and swollen with need until I'm almost humping his leg. When he finally softens in my mouth, he shoves me away and I land heavily on my ass, spluttering and choking on the bitter taste of our cum and my blood.

"Get out of my sight, Sofia," he barks, tucking his flaccid cock away.

Terrified and confused, I scramble to my feet and dart from the room, biting down on the wails threatening to escape. I'm blinded by the tears that run down my face, clinging to my cheeks and cruelly mimicking the sticky flow of cum and my own sinful juices leaking from between my thighs.

He's breaking me, slowly but surely. Every day I'm here, I find myself succumbing more and more to the forbidden desire within my heart for a man I should run from instead of admire. The lines between sanity and madness have been blurred ever since I found myself in that forest clearing on a stone seat, seeking release with my hand between my thighs to the photo of an anonymous stranger. But I know who he is, now. He's Pater...but more than that, he's Daddy.

Chapter Fifteen

I struggle to fully comprehend what happened back in the family room with Pater. He wanted me out of his sight as soon as he'd finished. *Did it mean so little to him?* I'm shocked by the strangeness of the inappropriate feelings he evokes in me combined with the wrongness of the whole situation. His initial response to my confession was unexpected, but his subsequent actions stunned me. Shame swirls in the pit of my stomach when I think about the way I responded to him and his touch. I shouldn't want him at all, let alone enjoy what he did to me.

Hurrying back to my room, I wince and whimper at the soreness radiating from my core as I move. Pater's words swim into my mind, about how he's going to get me pregnant, and I smother a sob with my hand. I rush into my bedroom and quietly close the door behind me before flinging myself onto my bed.

What have I gotten myself into? This isn't what I expected to find when I went looking for my real daddy, but I suppose at least I can say that I found him, and now I understand why my mom ran from him with me still inside her. *Fuck! What if he does get me pregnant?* I came here for a family, and it seems he's going to give me more of one than I bargained for.

Curling up under the covers, I close my eyes to the horrors of the day and the tumultuous emotions waging war inside me. Sleep eventually takes me, drawing my conscious mind away into dreams filled with Pater's dark eyes and commanding voice. Even in my sleep, his presence consumes me, demanding a respect he's never earned, but I find myself wanting to give it, in spite of my mind protesting against him.

I wake the following morning after an uneasy, restless sleep. My entire body aches, and my pussy is still throbbing and sore. It's earlier than I've been waking since my arrival here, but considering the previous morning's incident, and how I skipped out on the rest of the day apart from the evening meal, it's probably for the best. Not wanting to linger in bed and get caught shirking my share of the chores again, I slowly rise and get dressed. Every muscle feels taut and strained like I did a workout followed by a damn marathon. *Surely, I shouldn't be this uncomfortable?*

As I pull on my clothes at a snail's pace, groaning every time I bend and stretch, I notice the dark bruising on my hips and faint marks between my legs from where Pater held me as he fucked me. For once, my body doesn't heat when I think about him. I'm not sure if my foolish delusion has been shattered or if I'm still in shock after yesterday. I don't even want to contemplate the potential consequence of what happened, but I know for the next few weeks it's going to lurk in the back of my mind, taunting and teasing my sanity.

Shaking off the cloud that's settled in my mind with the heaviness of my thoughts, I head to the kitchen to help Vaughn. As usual, he's already started the chores. He refuses to meet my gaze, and I'm not sure how much he heard yesterday, but Pater and I were far from subtle or quiet. I can almost hear and feel the guttural scream of pain that ripped from my throat when Pater thrust into me for my very first time. *I mustn't think about it.* No matter how much discomfort I'm in, or how fresh the bruises are, blossoming all over my body, I refuse to think about it. A father's love is supposed to be gentle and kind, but his is raw, animalistic, and frighteningly cold.

"Morning, Vaughn," I say, my voice falsely bright.

He glances up at me and mumbles, "Morning." Then, he turns away again and focuses intently on the task of making breakfast.

I step up next to Vaughn, grab the dishes, and start to set the table, the two of us working together in absolute silence. It's almost too much to bear, but the routine chore is oddly calming, and I find it more soothing than maddening. I need a calm, constant presence in my chaotic life, and even with his refusal to strike up a conversation, whether he intends it or not, Vaughn is giving me just that.

There's no pressure when I'm with Vaughn, no need to try and impress him. I can only assume he's lived his whole life under Pater's roof, and in many ways, I envy him that experience. I think I'd rather have been under Pater's tyrannical rule than living with Gregory and his love affair with alcoholism.

"Morning, Eloy," I say softly, when my younger brother walks into the room, and he smiles back at me.

"Morning, Sofia."

It doesn't take long before everything is ready, but we've only just finished when Pater walks into the room and sits down at the head of the table. There's a shit-eating grin on his face when he notices the three of us sitting wordlessly, waiting for him.

"Well, would you look at that? Now, that's what I call progress. Looks like your little lesson yesterday is actually sinking in, Sofia," he comments, looking between us kids, and chuckling softly.

Vaughn's head stays down, his gaze forcibly fixed on the bowl in front of him. Eloy looks frightened and doesn't say anything. I don't know whether to answer or not, and I glance as subtly as I can toward my eldest brother, and he moves his head in an almost imperceptible nod.

"Yes, Pater," I agree, hating how meek I sound.

I'm unable to summon any of the fire I've previously displayed to him. While I know a little of what Pater's like, I've only had a few weeks of living under his roof, and realize all too well that I've barely scratched the surface of what he's truly capable of. He exhales a laugh, and nods appreciatively before settling down to eat. I wait for Vaughn's signal and follow his lead like I wish I'd done yesterday when to my own detriment, I ignored his advice.

"Kid, you should fill your sister in on the rest of the rules as well as the consequences of breaking them to make sure we don't have any more fuckups." Pater addresses Vaughn, leveling him with a stern frown. "I'm not as stupid as you kids think I am, so don't try anything," he warns, looking between the three of us before he gets up from the table and leaves the kitchen.

Does he know that Vaughn slipped out yesterday, and that he's been helping me find my feet while I adjust to this new life?

Chapter Sixteen

The sound of the truck engine revving jolts me out of my daydream, and I glance up at Vaughn to gauge his reaction. His usually tense shoulders relax, and his perpetually worried expression eases.

"He'll be gone for a few hours," he confirms as he rises to his feet and slips from the family room, where we're now sitting, and heads back into the kitchen.

Curious about what he's up to and not wanting to be alone, I follow him. I don't want to be left on my own to dwell on everything: the past, my memories, my thoughts, desires, and most of all, my fears. He may not fill the long silences with chatter, neither of the boys do, but Vaughn's presence, in particular, is a comfort to me...he makes me feel less isolated.

I've not asked Vaughn why he fears Pater so

much more than I do. His expression when I opened my mouth to ask, on one of my first days here, warned me not to go there. I suppose in some ways, I have my answer, but the true extent of the darkness residing in this place continues to remain a mystery.

I walk into the kitchen to find Vaughn buttering bread. I watch in silence as he makes a sandwich, selects a piece of fruit from the pantry, and wraps it all up in a cloth napkin before grabbing a small bottle of water from the fridge. Apart from looking at me every now and then, he doesn't acknowledge my presence with words. He slides the bolt across on the back door and walks out of the house into the empty yard beyond.

"Don't wander off," Vaughn says, making me jump. I wasn't expecting him to speak. "If you're planning on following me, stay close."

I do as he says, walking just a few steps behind him as he leads me around the house to what appears to be an old well; it's without a roof or bucket and covered by a board made of wooden slats. He's still clutching the parcel of food, and I wonder if he intends to throw it down there. *Won't Pater be mad that he's stealing and wasting food?* He beckons me closer, and I step up beside him. Curious, I lean over and peer through gaps in the wooden slats into the darkness below.

"Is there someone down there?" I ask him in

horror, clutching his arm and straining my eyes to see.

"Jocelyn, it's me, Vaughn. I've brought you some food," he calls, and I hear a rustle of movement from below us when he slips the parcel between the slats and drops it into the well.

I exhale sharply at his words, and his eyes don't leave mine even as my gaze flickers between him and the shadowy pit. It looks like I'm finally meeting the mysterious Jocelyn. She doesn't seem willing to speak, and it hits me again how quiet the house always is with the lack of chatter. The only sounds come from those of us living there when we're moving around. Vaughn leads me away from the pit and Jocelyn, no doubt sensing I'm about to break Pater's rules and bombard him with questions…but our daddy isn't here to listen to me ask them. *So there's no way he'll know, right?*

"What is that place? Why is she down there, Vaughn? How long has she been down there? What other rules was Pater telling you to fill me in on?" I interrogate.

The questions spill from my lips one after the other in a torrent as I try to rein in my horror but fail to stem the flood.

"That place is the oubliette, and Jocelyn is down there because she repeatedly defies Pater. She takes the punishment so that he doesn't punish me and

Eloy, not that it's ever stopped him..." he trails off, and my blood turns to ice.

"You mean?" I ask hesitantly, and when he glares at me, I leave the question unfinished because his look tells me everything I need to know.

"I should leave. We both should leave and never come back," I tell him, clutching his arm again, trying to stop him from going back into the house.

"Where would we go? You've not been here for long, and you don't understand what he's like beyond what you've seen already. Pater would find us. He wouldn't rest knowing his kids are out there without him. It won't work, and I'm not leaving without Eloy or Jocelyn. We don't have time to get her out of the oubliette today, and even if we did, it would be a few days before she'd be strong enough to leave. You came here and found us, and now you're one of us...running away won't change that," he says, pulling his arm out of my grip and carrying on toward the house.

I look back at the pit where our sister resides in the black belly of the earth. I let out a regretful sigh before following him inside. I don't like the thought of her being down there, but I think what surprises me the most is how seemingly unaffected Vaughan is by it. I suspect he's hiding his own rage and help-lessness, yet I can't help wondering how much of this is the norm for him.

I enter through the back door into the kitchen,

hoping to continue speaking to Vaughn, but he's already disappeared into his room, and Eloy is nowhere to be seen. My shoulders slump, and I hope I haven't upset my tentative ally. Even though he's not particularly forthcoming, he's still helped me and looked out for me when I've been around Pater. His words fill me with a warmth that's been absent for a long time, but equally fills me with a sense of foreboding. *'Now you're one of us.'*

Chapter Seventeen

As I close the backdoor behind me, I hear the rumble of an engine drawing nearer, and my heart stutters nervously in my chest. Pater's back already. Not wanting to get caught hanging around, I swiftly exit the kitchen, dart down the hallway, and head for my bedroom. I make it inside and shut the door just as I hear the front door being opened then closed, followed by the heavy footsteps of Pater as he walks through the house. I spend the rest of the day holed up in my room until it's time for dinner when I reluctantly leave to go and help Vaughn.

Over the next few weeks, or at least, I think a few weeks have passed…it's almost impossible to keep track of the days here, I settle into a regulated routine. I hate how I constantly feel like I'm treading on eggshells around Pater, though. I'm so conflicted about everything I've learned and experienced since I ran from Gregory and found myself practically standing on my daddy's doorstep. All the feelings that had started to grow within my tormented heart haven't faded, but now they're smothered by the constant worry and fear that envelopes me inside this house.

Tonight, as on many previous nights, I'm lying in bed, listening to the sounds of moans and cries of pleasure and pain echoing through the house. Pater's heavy grunts ring in my ears as I fight to tamper down the residual desire they awaken in me. I now know who he takes upstairs, even though I've yet to meet her face to face. It seems Jocelyn spends more time in the oubliette than above the ground, and when she isn't hidden in the earth, she's upstairs being fucked by Pater in one of the rooms we're forbidden to enter. My heart goes out to the sister I've never met.

I sob quietly as I touch myself to their animal-istic sounds, and I remember in the quiet darkness how it felt to be the one receiving his attention. *I shouldn't be doing this.* I tell myself the same thing over and over again, but as her cries reach the pitch of ecstasy, I feel the heat roll through me like a slow tide as I sully my soul and my body in which his blood flows.

The silence that follows the sound of their fucking drags on, and I lie awake, staring up at the dark ceiling. I'm being swept away by my own treacherous thoughts, and while I lie in the blackness, shivering through the aftershocks of my orgasm, I make a decision that will either free me or doom me forever.

Slipping out of my bed, I wince at the coolness of the temperature hitting my heated, flushed skin. I grab the backpack I still have slung over the bedpost and start pulling clothes from the drawers and shoving them inside. I can't stay here, and if I sneak out in the middle of the night, I might have a chance of getting away permanently. I don't know where I'll go, but if I remain here, I fear I'll fall victim to the madness running through me. Away from this house, the insanity can't touch me...and neither can he.

Not wanting to waste any time, I hurriedly pull on panties, a sweater over my sleep shirt, leggings, and finally a pair of shoes. The longer I delay, the more likely I am to get caught. Without giving myself time to think about what will happen if he catches me, I swing my bag over my shoulders, take a deep breath, and carefully open the bedroom door, partway. Peering through the gap into the hallway, I listen for a sign that anyone is awake. The stillness of the night and an empty corridor greet me, and I tiptoe through the opening and make my way toward the kitchen. The back door will grant me the easiest escape because I can flee into the deep forest beyond the edges of the yard.

I can see the door from where I'm standing, shrouded in shadow, in the hallway. The weight of the bag on my shoulders and the feel of it sitting against my back reassures me that I'm really going to do this, and this isn't some ill-fated dream or illusion of freedom. Steeling myself, I sneak into the kitchen, taking care not to make any noise. For once, the lack of personal touches and furnishings in the house are a blessing; I don't have to worry about tripping or knocking anything over as I inch closer and closer to the door that will grant me salvation.

I've only moved a few feet, but by the time I reach the door, my palms feel clammy and my heart is thumping so hard it feels as though it's about to burst out of my chest. No time for doubt now, though. I've gotten this far, and the longer I dilly-dally, the more likely I'll be caught. I grip the cold metal handle, and carefully twisting it, I open the door. A light breeze brushes against my face, and I glance behind me, just once, before stepping out into the night. I smile up at the black sky, pinpricked with a smattering of stars, and inhale deeply. It's time to go.

I start walking, retracing the steps I took to get here on that first day. I try not to think about my sister trapped in the pit as I approach the edge of the yard. Vaughn said she wouldn't be strong enough to run with us, so I've made the choice to leave them all behind, even though it makes my soul ache to do so. I'll come back and save them, but first I need to save myself from this fate.

I take my first step across the boundary of trees encircling the house and yard. I stumble through the forest, trying not to trip over roots and fallen foliage. I don't have a flashlight, the batteries in that and my phone have long since died, not that I'd be able to get a signal, anyway. We're well and truly cut off out here. A twig snaps, the crack seems as loud as gunshot, making me jump. I whip around and scan the thicket of trees for a sign of someone being there, fearing that Pater might be behind me, then laugh to myself when I don't see anything. *It was just my imagination. My fear playing tricks on me.*

I break through the trees into the clearing with the stone chair and pause, heart hammering in my chest as my blood freezes in my veins. Sitting in the chair like he belongs there, one leg crossed over the other, leaning forward, and with his chin resting on his hand, is Pater.

Chapter Eighteen

"Running away are you, Sofia?" It sounds more like an observation than a question.

"N-no," I stammer, already knowing I'm caught. *How did he know?*

"I want to believe you, I really do, Sofia."

He sighs dramatically, sounding like an aggrieved parent scolding his child as he gets to his feet and approaches me. I'm frozen, stock still, frantically willing myself to move my legs and run. But in a few short strides, he's standing in front of me, his shadowed features and large frame blotting out the stars as he towers over me, and my chance to escape is lost.

"But, once again, you've chosen to break the fucking rules. First you run, abandoning your family, then you try to deny it, and here we are, back where I first found you. I'm becoming convinced you *want* to be punished, Sofia," he says, tilting his head thoughtfully to one side.

I don't answer, and I don't move, even as he lifts his hand to gently sweep the loose strands of my hair out of my face and brushes his fingers down my cheek. The rough pad of his thumb caresses lightly over my skin, leaving a trail of fire in its wake. I swallow back the whimper of terror as a tear slips free. I don't know what I want anymore, but I'm not sure this is it. His other hand reaches around to grab my backpack, and sliding it off my shoulders, he drops it to the ground. I reach out for it, but he seizes my hand in his much larger one and leads me toward the chair.

"What are you doing?" I protest, shrieking when he lifts me from the ground and swiftly pulls off my leggings and panties before setting me down in the seat, still warm from when he was sitting there.

"What I should've done when I first saw you sitting here with your fingers buried in your sweet little pussy and you told me you were mine. I'm going to make you my wife," he growls, palming me over my panties I'm still wearing as he crashes his mouth down over mine.

I beat my fists against his chest, fighting desperately, but he only chuckles into my mouth. He grips my wrists in one of his hands as the other one shoves my shirt and sweater up and divests me of my underwear, leaving my pussy bare and exposed to the night breeze and to him. He doesn't hesitate, dipping his fingers into my body while expertly working my clit until I'm whimpering and grinding against him. *No! What am I doing?!* He swallows my cries of pleasure, thrusting his tongue deep into my open mouth to tangle with mine.

"It's time to make you mine again and remind you of who you belong to," Pater smirks as I shudder through the delirium of ecstasy, and he lowers his pants, releasing his thick cock.

I struggle against him, awareness and clarity returning in a split second, but I'm incapable of fighting him. Lowering my body so my ass is on the edge of the chair, he spreads my legs wide, lines himself up with my pussy and jerks his powerful hips forward, filling me to the hilt. My scream splits the air, and his groan of satisfaction reverberates through my soul, tearing me in two.

Pater fucks me slowly, taking his time to fill me completely with every thrust of his hips. He ignores my cries of pain, seeking only to fulfil his own needs and gorge on his pleasure until he's satisfied. He lowers his head to kiss me again, dominating me with his mouth as he fucks me into a bittersweet oblivion. His kiss is filled with lust and when he grinds against my clit, I lose myself to the darkness of the sensations he's arousing, and as my pussy pulses around his cock, my mind floats on clouds around me. I'm brought back down to earth by

Pater jerking roughly against me as he once again spills his seed within my unprotected body.

Pater's body is heavy, the rigid muscles of his abdomen are pressed almost flat against mine, and his cock is still twitching inside me. When he lifts his head to look down at my face, his hot breath blows against my skin, and his expression is a mix of elation blurring with a deep satisfaction, but both are overshadowed by the possessive grin he's directing straight at me. Pater kisses my lips again, softly this time, and then presses another gentle, fatherly kiss to my forehead, his stubble scratching at my skin.

I stare up at him in shock, my legs still spread wide and his softening erection still buried deep inside me. He pulls out, and I slide from the chair and its plinth to the cold earth. I can feel the twigs and small stones digging into my uncovered skin as I sit there while his cum slips slowly from my body, running down the seam of my ass to pool on the ground beneath me.

I'm finding it almost impossible to process what we just did and the fact that, once again, Pater's come inside me. My daddy, the man who sired me, is purposefully trying to get me pregnant. He warned me before, but when he didn't touch me again after that first time, I didn't think he meant it. *How fucking wrong I was.* I've tried to run but failed, and I'm afraid of what else he may do to me now.

Although, I can't think of anything worse than him succeeding in his mission to fill my womb with his child. *This is so fucking wrong.* It's the farthest thing from anything I could've imagined when I first laid eyes on him, knowing who he was to me.

"Come on, Sofia. Naughty children don't go unpunished. It's time you understood where the bad girls go when they tell lies and break the rules. I told you I know everything that happens under my roof. Yet you *still* chose to go against me. *Tut tut*, well now it's time to face the consequences of your actions."

I'm hauled unceremoniously onto my unsteady feet, and I barely manage to snag the strap of my backpack before Pater begins dragging me along. I stumble helplessly behind him until we break through the tree line and reach the yard. When he bypasses the house and pulls me toward the pit, the oubliette, which I can see is uncovered, I claw at his hand, frantically trying to pry his fingers loose.

"Please don't put me in there, Pater. Please! I promise to be good! I'm sorry, Daddy!" I wail, but he shakes his head.

"You haven't learned your lesson yet. You don't appreciate how easy I've been on you up until now. You need to understand your place and stop acting like a petulant kid, defying me every single time my back is turned. A few days in the hole ought to reinforce the lesson you seem determined not to grasp. Maybe you'll gain a little more respect for the rules of my house. *You* chose to find *me*, and you don't get to run away now, just because it suits *you*. That's not how this family works, Sofia," he says harshly, chiding me.

Pater sweeps me off my feet, and I scream as I'm suspended over the hole in the ground. It looks like the open mouth to hell, waiting to swallow me whole.

"Please!" I beg, clutching tightly onto him, tears streaming down my face, as he lowers me inside before releasing me and letting me fall into the depths of the abyss.

Chapter Nineteen

I should've listened to Vaughn, and I shouldn't have tried to run. Of course, Pater knew what I would attempt to do; he's made it very clear that nothing goes unnoticed by him in that house. I don't know whether Vaughn told on me, or if Pater somehow read the thoughts swirling through my mind. Regardless of how he found out, this is where running got me.

The floor of the pit is padded with thick straw, no doubt there to cushion the fall. Jocelyn is notice-ably absent, and maybe that's a good thing for her. Vaughn told me she spends an awful lot of time down here, but I'm not sure being up there in the house will be that much better for her.

I'm glad I managed to grab my backpack when Pater hauled me out of that clearing and dumped me in this godforsaken hole. At least, I've got some extra clothing, so I'm able to dress a little warmer. I still have no panties on, and the remnants of mine and Pater's cum still clings to my inner thighs, but there's not much I can do about that right now. I pull on some spare clothes from my backpack, grateful for the added layers. I notice my dead phone, and I once again lament the fact I left my charger at home in my rush to escape. Even though there's no signal around here. it would've provided a little light and a way to track the hours and days ahead of me. I curl up tightly into a ball for warmth and settle on the straw as best I can, and using my bag as a pillow, I try to get some sleep.

Hours later I jolt awake. Somehow, I managed to drift off, but I have no way to gauge how much time has passed since I landed down here. I stretch as much as the limited space will allow before I slowly get to my feet on aching bones and muscles. The light at the top of the hole seems a little brighter, so I'm guessing it's morning now.

I wait for someone to come, for Vaughn maybe, but I'm left alone. I'm down in the dark with no food and no light, save the small pinprick of daylight trickling down through slats in the covering over the top of the hole. Vaughn warned me what would happen if I broke the rules. I didn't listen...but Daddy always knows, and now I'm paying penance for my mistakes.

There's nothing to do but sit in the still emptiness of the oubliette, surrounded by the smooth walls and hay-strewn floor. I sit against the wall, leaning on it with my knees bent and my arms wrapped around them. The heaviness of my heart and the pangs in my stomach remind me I'm alive, and I'm not the shell I sometimes feel I've become. The only glimpse of a silver lining is the utter peace and tranquility I find in this narrow chute whenever my fruitless pleas and screams for freedom aren't bouncing around its walls.

Shadows dance on the sides of the shaft as daylight fades, looking like monsters coming to devour me as their tainted sacrifice. Night falls, plunging me into an all consuming blackness, and the surrounding walls begin to feel like they're closing in. But the only way out is up, and the prospect of freedom is too far out of reach. The sound of a breeze I can't feel whispers overhead, rustling the leaves on the trees in the nearby forest. Sunlight might peek down like a naughty child at a keyhole during the day, but at night, the darkness and the stone walls draw out the heat, leaving nothing for me. As I curl up tighter, shivering against the chill of the pit, regret swirls in my head at my foolishness in thinking I could evade Pater. *Why did I run?*

I'm losing track of time, but I'm sure no more than a couple of days have passed. Occasionally, a bottle of water is lowered into the oubliette, delivered by an anonymous hand. I'm feeling the lack of food, and I'm freezing cold when the sun isn't shining down on my pitiful form, curled up on the straw.

The only things keeping me from losing my mind in the narrow confines of my prison is the thought of getting out and the face of my mom, now blurred in my memory. It's mostly too dark to see the photos still buried in the bottom of my back-pack, but even when the sun is high enough over-head, and its taunting light trickles in and dances on my skin, I'm too afraid to look at them because I know who'll be staring up at me.

"Sofia," a hushed voice calls out my name, and I squint up blearily to see who it is.

It's hard to tell, but I'm almost certain it's Vaughn; his voice doesn't have the edge that Pater's does.

"Vaughn! Please, can you get me out?" I plead, praying he'll say yes.

"No. I'm sorry. I can't go against him. Not this time," he admits, sounding apologetic.

The response confirms it is Vaughn standing above me. He's annoyingly far away, but at least he's here.

"How did you manage to come and see me?"

"Pater's gone out, so I snuck some food and extra water for you. It's not much, but it'll keep you going for now."

He blots out the light as he squeezes the parcel of food through a gap in the cover, like he did for Jocelyn, and then lets it go. I watch it fall, and somehow manage to catch it before it hits the floor. The smell of bread and butter assaults me, and I crouch down on the floor, hurriedly opening the package and setting the bottle of water aside for after I've eaten.

"Thank you, Vaughn," I whisper, and my voice must carry because he nods in response to my thanks.

"I've gotta go. If I'm caught out here, then we'll both end up down there. I'll see you soon I hope," he says, and his face vanishes from my view.

I hope so too.

I ravenously attack the sandwich Vaughn brought for me before eagerly devouring the small apple that was also in the parcel, groaning in satisfaction at the simple joy of eating. I hate that I'm so dirty, but I'm too hungry to care. Feeling better than I have since I greeted the bottom of this hole, I lie down and let the rest of the day pass in a haze of light slumber and bursts of wakefulness. The boredom and restriction of movement is what's wearing me down the most, and I hope Pater forgives me soon and lets me out. I don't know how much more of this I can take before I lose my mind.

I'm just slipping into another doze when a scraping above me draws my attention. I look up as a familiar face peers over the edge of the oubliette. Pater stares down at me and smiles when he sees me looking back up at him.

"Have you decided whether you're going to follow the rules yet, or do you need another few days in the hole?"

"Pater, please let me out. I'll be good, Daddy," I beg, hoping he'll let me out of this place.

"How do I know you're being sincere, Sofia? This isn't the first time you've broken your promise to behave. How do I know you aren't trying to hustle your way outta there?" he questions, his lips tilting deviously into a smirk, no doubt enjoying my vulnerability and discomfort.

I'm completely at his mercy, and if he chooses to leave me to rot down here, there's nothing I can do to stop him.

"Please! I promise, I'll behave myself. I'm not lying to you," I cry, my voice cracking from the overwhelming fear that he'll walk away any minute.

I'm not sure how long he stands there watching me break down in front of him, but as always, time seems to slow when he's around. Every moment with him is drawn out, purposeful, so when he finally throws a rope ladder down the hole, it almost seems to fall in slow motion before the end of it tumbles to a stop at my waist.

"Hurry up, or I'll throw the whole ladder down there while you're still climbing it," he threatens.

I jump to my feet, scoop up my bag, and climb as fast as I can. Soon enough, I'm hauling myself out of the top, inhaling the cool fresh air in large gulps as I try to slow my racing heart. That was exhausting, and had Vaughn not snuck me some food when he did, I don't know that I'd have had the energy to make it out by myself.

I'm sprawled on the ground at Pater's feet, and in this moment as I stare up at him with tears in my eyes, I've never felt more like a child, worshipping the ground he walks on with fear of the repercussions if I don't. My stint in the hole has weakened my resolve, and I'm too fragile to fight against his wishes. Pater is my daddy, and I'm his daughter, and for now, I'll obey his rules.

Chapter Twenty

Pater doesn't move to help me up or assist me in getting back to the house. But I'm guessing, the way he sees it, I got myself into this mess, and now I've faced the consequence, it's time for me to pick myself up and get on with it. He's not about to coddle me or offer me any comfort when I'm the one who fucked up. It doesn't change what he did to me, and it doesn't make it okay, but maybe, someday, it will make me strong enough to accept this fate or fight it.

Slowly, when I feel ready, I push myself up onto my hands and knees and try to stand on shaking legs. What little energy I had, I expended it in my urgency to escape the oubliette. Pater disappears into the house, and after a few moments, I see Vaughn in the doorway watching me struggle. An unfamiliar young woman, who I'm assuming is Jocelyn, is standing beside him. She glances behind her before she shoves him toward me and then disappears. Vaughn rushes over, and helping me to stand, he hustles me into the house and sets me down on one of the chairs in the kitchen before closing the back door.

I groan, leaning back on the chair. After spending a few days on the oubliette floor, my stiff muscles and joints are reluctant to bend and stretch to accommodate a normal sitting position. The straw provided some cushioning, but it wasn't exactly comfortable.

"Thanks," I mumble, folding my hands in my lap.

I feel disgusting, and I desperately need to have a shower and wash the grime off, not to mention put on a fresh set of clothing. Vaughn sets down a glass of water on the table next to me and leaves me alone in the room. I watch the beads of condensation slide down the sides to pool around its base, and I think about how I feel like that water; malleable and bending to the will of the vessel shaping it and restrained by the hard exterior holding it in place, just like Pater does to me and the rest of his family... *my family*.

I'm afraid of the future, and what lies ahead should I continue to stay here with him. I promised to be good, to behave and do what he asks of me, but I'm still so unsure. Every piece of truth I've uncovered has thrown filthy secrets into a harsh light, and I can't help questioning everything I've ever thought and wanted. Nothing here is black and white. Everything is a murky shade of gray, and I fear my soul will never be clean again.

I finish the water and place the empty glass down on the wooden table with a small clunk. Getting to my feet, I slowly make my way through the house to the bathroom. I need a shower and to put on some clean clothes. I feel disgusting, and I'm sure I look and smell equally bad after my ordeal. I still don't know how many days have passed since I was imprisoned in the oubliette, and honestly, I'm not sure I want to know. I don't want to be able to put a timestamp on the cruelty of my punishment.

The hallway is empty, but I can hear the sound of voices coming from the family room up ahead. Maybe when I'm clean, I'll join them. More likely, though, I'll hide away in my room and sleep the memories away.

Stripping out of my clothes, I ball them up to put them in the trash. After living in them constantly for the last few days, they're completely ruined. I gaze at my reflection in the mirror, taking in my dirt-covered skin, my lank, filthy hair, and pale complexion. There are dark rings around my eyes, and looking closer, I notice the hollow quality has returned to them that was there after I found Mom in the bathtub with her wrists sliced open, dripping blood onto the shower mat. She fucking abandoned me and left me alone with Gregory. She chose to take her own life rather than spend it with me. I don't know how much time has passed since Mom died, but the longing that led me to this house hasn't been dulled, it's just been cast into shadow by the imposing father of us all.

I let the hot water loosen and relax my aching muscles as I wash away the grime from my skin. The longer I stand there, soaking in the water, I think about everything that's happened and the family I've found. I understand why Mom tried to hide them from me, but it doesn't change the fact they are mine, and I belong to them. Their blood flows in my veins, and we are bound together by the man who created us. I don't hate him, even after everything he's done to me, but it's only now, as I reflect on these things, I realize that I love him. It's bizarre, it's terrifying, and it's wrong, but even though I shouldn't, the feeling's there like a small spark inside me.

I continue to stand under the spray long after my body is clean, enjoying the heat and the feel of the water running over my skin. I know I can't hide in here forever, and I don't want to get into trouble for using all the hot water. But the thought that scares me the most is that I'm not sure why I'm hiding or who I'm hiding from; Pater or myself.

Chapter Twenty-One

Stepping out of my bedroom the next morning, I halt when I see the young woman standing in the hallway. I know from our brief encounter yesterday this is Jocelyn. She can't be much older than me, but her eyes tell another story altogether. I can tell she's seen and experienced more than I could ever begin to imagine.

She doesn't say anything, just silently appraises me with a sad expression on her face. Our eyes lock and her sharp intake of breath makes my heart jump. I know exactly what she's seeing when she looks into my eyes because it's the same thing I see in hers...*him*.

I glance away, heat rising in my cheeks. I'm not sure why her reaction surprised me. Sometimes, if I caught Mom unawares, she'd do the same thing; she'd flinch, but it was always fleeting before she'd mask it. I never noticed it when I was young, but as I grew older I wondered why until I confronted her about it one day, and she admitted that I had my daddy's eyes. I never understood why they bothered her so much until I met him and felt his gaze piercing through me.

I don't say anything to break the silence that feels like a vast expanse between us, and when it seems clear she isn't going to either, I turn to head for the family room.

"Vaughn cares about his family. Don't break that trust. He's a good kid," Jocelyn finally says, and I turn to face her.

Her expression is haunted, and I wonder what exactly put that hollow pain in her eyes, but when she blinks, it clears, and her expression becomes impassive. I get the feeling Jocelyn is used to masking her emotions from those around her, and I'm guessing, from one person in particular. However, given what Vaughn told me, and what she said just now, she has a fierce protective streak in her, and I can see that same quality reflected in Vaughn every time he's tries to help me avoid getting into trouble.

I have no words to say to her in response, but I nod in acknowledgement. I can't promise anything when I'm still drowning in my own confusion about my place here. I think this is the only acceptance I will get from her, and that's enough.

"Thank you for helping me yesterday," I tell her sincerely, and her face relaxes a little, but the tension never leaves her shoulders.

"I look out for my family. What kind of mother or sister would I be if I didn't?" she asks, but it sounds rhetorical, so I don't answer

The familial ties are strong in this household, and I can feel them drawing me closer into their embrace. I don't know whether I should submit or continue to struggle against them. I shed my mother's name when I walked out of her door after she abandoned me, and in that moment, I became a Greene and stepped into this family as Pater's daughter. This is my family now, and I chose them over everything that came before.

"Vaughn told me what happened. I don't blame you for trying to run," she says.

"How much did he tell you?" I ask, wondering what else Vaughan shared with her. My mind flashes back to the night he walked in on me pleasuring myself and prevented me from getting caught.

"Enough to know that you'll never be able to escape this family's legacy, even if you do manage to get out of here." Jocelyn frowns thoughtfully and then pulls me into the bathroom.

"What are you doing?" I ask as she rummages in a small cupboard for something.

"How long have you been here now?"

"A few weeks, I think. I'm not sure exactly. Why?"

"Have you had a period since you arrived?"

My blood freezes, and my heart stops dead in my chest as I stare at her,

"No, but that doesn't mean anything. I've always been irregular. What about you? How come you've not had any children yet?" I probe.

"I'm not sure, but I hope I never do. The boys were like my children until I ruined it."

"Ruined it? What do you mean?"

Her eyes fill with a sheen of tears before hardening, but her voice is thick with emotion when she finally answers, "Eloy has gone to where evil can't touch him again, and Vaughn is never going to forgive me for what I allowed to happen."

My heart halts at her words, and a tear rolls down my face as I picture my quiet youngest brother who always seemed to be on the outskirts of everything. Jocelyn straightens up, and her expression says the subject is closed as she holds out a pregnancy test to me, but I shake my head.

"It's not been that long," I inform her. "I don't need that. It's not unusual for me to go several weeks without a period."

She doesn't seem convinced, but she reluctantly puts the test back in the cupboard.

" For your sake, I hope you're right. I still think you should take the test, but I won't force you."

"I'm fine," I reassure her, and she nods, accepting my response.

I can tell she's not happy that I refused, but I don't feel any different and doing the test would make this situation feel so much more real, no matter the result. I want the part of this that still feels like a dream to last for as long as possible. I don't want to sink any further into the nightmare, and I don't want to be woken up to discover this is my new reality.

Jocelyn exits the bathroom, leaving me standing there with the weight of my refusal hanging in the air, suffocating me with the knowledge of what it would mean if I'm wrong. I shake my head, attempting to clear the fog of thoughts swirling around inside it, and step into the now empty hallway. I can hear quiet voices filtering out of the family room, and I should go to them, but I find my feet leading me in the opposite direction, deeper into the house.

Chapter Twenty-Two

I hesitate for a split second, looking behind me only once before continuing. I can't say why I'm doing this, I'm bound to get caught, but I know that stopping isn't an option now I've started down this path. I get to the bottom of the stairs and pause, looking up at them. Suddenly they seem longer than they really are, and I wonder at my sanity for doing this, but curiosity has got the better of me. Inhaling deeply, I put a foot on the bottom step when I hear a voice hiss from behind me.

"No! Don't go up there!"

Running footsteps approach, and a warm hand grabs me by the elbow, pulling me back.

"Are you fucking insane? Don't go up there. If Pater finds out that you've gone up there, you don't know what he'll do," Jocelyn scolds, her voice heavy with fear beneath the warning tone.

"What will he do to me that he hasn't already?" I laugh hollowly.

She shakes her head, "Those are his special rooms, and we are not allowed to go in there without his express permission."

"Have you been in them?" I ask her bluntly.

"Not all of them. Pater is very private. I don't want to know what's in them, and we're forbidden to ask. Sometimes, I listen to my fear when it comes to Pater, and you should too," Jocelyn admits, biting her lip.

"I don't want to listen to it all the time. I want to fight back."

"Not on this," she replies bluntly and proceeds to pull me back down the hallway, her hand wrapped firmly around my arm.

I could free myself from her hold if I chose, but I let her lead me away from certain punishment and into the kitchen where the morning meal is being prepared. Not two minutes later, Pater walks into the room, and the tension ramps up by a thousand percent.

"No good morning for your dad, kids?" he says, raising an eyebrow as he looks between all three of us when we stare silently at him.

I surprise myself when I'm the first to respond, "Morning, Daddy."

He looks at me with his signature smirk firmly in place, and I fight the urge to squirm in my seat. It never fails to disarm me when he does that. It throws me back to a time when I had no idea who he was, and I almost wish in these moments that I still don't. The other two follow suit, and we all settle down into the familiar morning ritual, but now with the glaring absence of Eloy.

After we're done and everything has been cleaned up, Pater slides his chair back, scraping it along the floor as he moves to stand.

"Sofia, come with me," he instructs, and my stomach twists nervously.

I'm confused because I haven't broken any rules or done anything to warrant special attention, so I can't be about to be punished. I don't move at first as my mind whirs frantically, trying to figure out what he could possibly think I've done.

"Go on, it'll only be worse if you don't," Jocelyn whispers, urging me forward, worry splashed across her features.

My hands are shaking as I walk around the table toward Pater who then leads me out of the room. I expect him to take me into the family room like he's done before, but he bypasses it and the first floor bedrooms, and instead, he makes for the stairs. After what Jocelyn hinted at this morning, I want to turn tail and run, but he's already proven that he'll be one step ahead of me. Running is the worst thing I could do right now; he'd catch me before I could even finish the thought.

As if to prove my point and maybe sensing my conflict, Pater twists his head to glance over his shoulder with his eyebrow raised when I hesitate. I immediately start to follow him again as we move into the only part of the house I've not yet ventured. My lungs feel tight, and my heart is hammering in a rapid drumbeat against my ribs. I've been warned against going to these rooms, and when I started to head up here this morning, Jocelyn stopped me. *Why am I suddenly being invited here now?*

Once upstairs, I'm led down an unfamiliar hallway past a few closed doors, which have my curiosity rearing its head again, until finally Pater opens a door and walks inside what looks to be his bedroom. Nervously twisting my hands, I enter the room, and as I do, Pater shuts the door behind me. The click as the catch moves into place echoes in my ears.

Pater's hands touch my shoulders, making me jump, and his warm breath blows on my face as he chuckles in my ear at my reaction. I shiver reflexively and fight to repress the urge to lean into the hard body standing directly behind me.

"W-why am I up here?" I stammer, hating how afraid I sound while attempting to calm my frazzled nerves.

"You wanted to know what's up here. Well, Fia, I'm going to show you," Pater says matter-of-factly.

I spin around to face him, a soft gasp leaving my

mouth at his use of my nickname. I never told him about that, and I never mentioned wanting to know what was up here. Without giving me the chance to respond, he dips his head down and kisses me fully on the lips. The stubble on his chin scratches lightly at my skin, and the intense passion in his kiss ignites a reluctant heat in my belly.

I'm powerless and foolishly unwilling to stop him as he shoves me toward his bed and proceeds to remove every piece of my clothing until I'm completely naked and exposed.

"Good girl, now lie down and let me taste that pussy of yours before I fill it up," Pater instructs, and I obey his command, remembering how it felt when he fucked me before and Jocelyn's warning down in the kitchen.

When I feel his tongue probing my entrance, I let out a breathy moan. Pater's chuckle vibrates against my core, and I shudder at the sensation rolling through me. Heat floods down below as he slowly lavishes attention on my pussy, pushing his tongue inside until his mouth is pressed against me and my cries are filling his bedroom. This shouldn't feel so good, and I curse whatever part of me is broken enough to enjoy the sensations he's creating within me.

"Oh, God," I nearly scream the words when the orgasm sweeps me away on its riptide.

"My turn," Pater says, rising to his full height

and removing his clothes to reveal his taut body and the thick erection jutting out from his hips.

My body is still weak from the aftershocks of my orgasm, but I manage to move until I'm perched on the end of his bed and my face is level with his cock. I take a deep breath as he forces his cock past my parted lips, filling my mouth and throat in a steady rhythm and making me gag.

As his movements become jerky he pushes me back, so I'm lying down on the bed. I know what's expected of me, and I spread my legs open for him. He covers me with his heavy body, lines himself up with my pussy, and thrusts fully into me until I'm whimpering at the painful stretch from his cock. *No matter how many times he does this, I will never get used to the feeling of him taking me like this.*

His dark eyes are almost black, and his usually tidy black hair is messy, making the thin silver streaks more stark in the bright light streaming through the window. His hands are planted either side of my head and he proceeds to fuck me, raw and hard, until I'm panting, sweating, and chasing another illicit release. Our combined moans and the sound of our hips slapping together fill the narrow space between us, and I can feel my mind slipping away.

"That's it, Fia, let me fill you up," he groans, bringing me back to the reality of the moment.

He jerks his hips roughly against me, penetrating

me so deeply I cry out at the shock and sudden pain of it. Then he stops, shaking above me, with his cock buried fully inside my body as he spills his release.

Pater finally pulls out, and presses another soft kiss against my lips before bringing me crashing back to reality when he places his warm hand gently across my bare stomach and says, "I'm going to fill this belly of yours with my baby, Fia. But unlike your momma, you aren't going to run off with my child inside you. I'm going to watch you grow swollen with my child. You came to me looking for family, and what kind of father would I be if I didn't give my little girl what she wants?"

Chapter Twenty-Three

After dressing in a daze, I kiss Pater on the cheek and wander back down the stairs to the kitchen. Jocelyn and Vaughn are still in there, and they both look up when I enter. I'm not certain I could put into words what just happened if questioned, but neither of them ask, not even to check on my well-being. *It's sure as shit I'm not okay.* Jocelyn's expression is sympathetic as she quietly gives me a swift embrace, but Vaughn's emotions are less clear.

I don't know how long I was up there, and I don't need to ask if they know what just occurred; it's obvious that they do. If I can hear perfectly what Pater does to Jocelyn most nights, then they'll have heard everything.

I can still feel his touch all over my body, and the residual ache from where he took me so roughly. I know my lips are swollen, and I'm sure to carry the bruises of his passion on my skin by tomorrow. I might have enjoyed the feelings and the pleasure he gave me, in spite of the immorality of our actions, but hopefully, bruises are the only marks of his love I'll have to bear.

The rest of the day passes uneventfully, and I'm relieved when it's time to crawl into bed at nightfall. Once there, I toss and turn, though, unable to sleep. My mind refuses to rest, replaying everything that happened today and focusing on the terrifying scenario that could occur as a result.

More time passes, and I no longer care to track the days or try to figure out how many have passed since I arrived here. Since the morning Pater took me upstairs, I've found myself being fucked by him more regularly, either in my room whenever he comes to find me or taken to his bedroom again. I'm losing hope, and I'm losing another piece of myself each time I succumb to his touch.

Finally, I can't take anymore, and once again, I decide to break the chains binding me to this family. I wait until the middle of the night when everything is as still and quiet as death, and grabbing my back-pack, I prepare to leave. I must be insane for risking this all over again, especially so soon after being pulled out of the oubliette. I already love and care deeply for my family, even though I've not been here for very long, but I can't stay here anymore.

I always wanted to know where I came from,

and in succeeding, I found a twisted legacy with a daddy who's at the head of it all. I don't know how far this goes back, but I suspect Mom knew more than she would have liked, which is why she ran with me when she had the chance. I can't blame her for keeping it a secret from me, but I don't regret my decision to come here either. I should be reeling with disgust at everything I've discovered, but I'm not, and that scares me almost as much as the prospect of Pater successfully siring a child with me.

I slip out of my bedroom with more purpose than the last time. I'm determined to get out of here. I cringe at the thought of returning to the home I ran from, but Mom's house is the only other place I can think of going. I'd go to a friend's if I had any, but the lie I told Gregory about going to a sleepover was bigger than he knew; I haven't had any real friends in a long time. If I'm careful, I can sneak in and hide there for a few days. I doubt Gregory will be sober enough to notice I'm there. I'll only stay long enough to plan my next move, and while I'm there, I can grab some money and the stuff he forced me to leave behind when I ran. When I'm better prepared, I'll leave, once and for all, and start over somewhere new. I've no idea where I'll be at the end of all of this, but I'll worry about it once I've successfully gotten out of here.

I make my way stealthily through the house to

the back door, which I'm surprised to find is unlocked.

"Where are you going?"

The familiar voice stops me in my tracks, and I spin around to see Jocelyn standing in the kitchen doorway, watching me with her arms crossed. I tilt my head to one side and give her an imploring look.

"I can't stay here. I've tried. I'm sorry," I apologize, and she lets out a sigh.

"If you're going to go, you could've at least said goodbye to us," she says stiffly.

I listen carefully for any sound of Pater being aware of what's happening down here, and I drop my bag to the floor and quickly walk up to her and wrap my arms around her.

"I thought you'd try to stop me," I whisper in her ear.

"You're right, we would have, but I can tell it wouldn't have made any difference if we'd tried to talk you out of it. Short of telling Pater, there's little we could do to change your mind," she admits with a shrug when I let go and take a step back.

"Thank you for accepting my decision," I reply gratefully.

"If you're going to run, leave now. He'll be awake soon. I should warn you, though, running won't stop what's going to happen, and it won't erase those thoughts inside your head. Pater will find you, and he'll drag you back kicking and screaming when he does. I won't be able to save you from his temper."

"I wouldn't expect you to try, but I won't be found. Maybe if I run far enough, I'll be able to escape. I have to try. I want to hate him…I want to, but I can't find it in me," I confess, my voice cracking on the words.

"I hope for your sake he doesn't find you," Jocelyn says sadly, and turning away, she walks slowly out of the kitchen.

I stare after her for a moment, saying a silent goodbye to her departing figure. Then, shouldering my backpack more securely, I open the door and step out into the night. Ignoring the woodland path that led me to my previous damnation, I swing around the house past Pater's truck and aim straight for the dirt road and civilization. If I keep to the shadows and out of sight, then maybe I'll manage to escape from the hell threatening to drag me into its depths.

My soul feels heavy, forsaken by the cravings that have been plaguing me since I unknowingly looked at my daddy's photo. I'm still cursed with lust for the man who was once a stranger, but maybe this road can lead me to freedom from these immoral desires.

Chapter Twenty-Four

I take off down the road, not stopping to look back and check if I've been spotted. I don't want to see if his face is at the window, watching me run from him. He'd accuse me of abandoning my family, and he'd be right, but I'm saving myself from a fate of his choosing.

Darkness fades into light, and when the sun starts to creep up over the trees, I finally stop, needing a breather. I'm exhausted, but I had to put as much distance as possible between myself and the house where my family lies sleeping. They've yet to discover what I've done, except for Jocelyn that is. I don't expect her to cover for me, but I wonder if she'll admit to knowing anything. I imagine she'll keep quiet, if only to protect herself. I somehow doubt that Pater will be forgiving or lenient with her if he knows she let me go and didn't rush to wake him.

As the day wears on, my stomach starts to grumble, but I ignore it. I'm hoping to pick up some food in the town where I found Gregory's bat shit crazy momma. Knowing what I do now, I'm guessing she's probably my aunt, making Gregory my cousin...honestly, I'd prefer not to be related to either of them. Gregory's snide remark about fucking family makes more sense now, although I wish it didn't. I was happy in my ignorant bubble of lust, not knowing that the man I desired so badly was my daddy.

In the grand scheme of things, though, my ignorance wouldn't have made any difference. Pater wanted me to be his wife and the mother of his child, and it didn't matter to him that I was his fully fledged daughter...in fact, it mattered more to him that I am his blood because it meant I belonged to him completely. I shake off the thoughts taking over, knowing if I don't, I'll never be able to stop myself from spinning around and venturing down the road leading to the hell that is the Greene family home and Pater.

"I hate him! I hate Pater. I hate my daddy!" I scream the words out loud into the emptiness of the trees on either side of the road.

The words are a lie, and they taste bitter like ash on my tongue, choking me on the falsehood I dared to utter. Tears start to fall, and I wrap my arms around my body to stop myself from crumbling where I stand. I can hide the truth from Pater and my siblings, but I can't lie to myself about what's in my heart. I love Jocelyn and Vaughn, like the brother and sister they are, and Eloy too, but I'm also cursed because I feel the wrong kind of love for the man who is as much a part of me as my mom. *Is this how she felt, when she ran away pregnant with me? Did she see the horrors I've seen and feel the same conflict I do?* The thought cracks my already fragile heart in two, and I'm not sure I can endure much more before it's destroyed completely. Love is confusing; it's painful, and it makes me want to rip out my heart just to cure myself of the disease that's overtaken it

I swipe away my tears with the back of my hand, compose myself as best I can, and start moving again. I can't afford to stop and fall to pieces, not out here where I'm so exposed and there's a chance Pater will find me. I laugh at the irony of the fact that the last time I was trekking down this road, I was fleeing from my stepdad and the emptiness of a home without my mom in it, but now the tables have turned. The difference is that I'm running from family, not the illusion of family that my mom tried so desperately to create for me with Gregory. The facade was always clear to my eyes, but I never understood why she stayed with him, especially after he took up drinking and let his temper loose.

The sun is high in the sky by the time I reach the outskirts of the town, but I decide not to stop, just in case I'm spotted by Gregory's momma, or Pater comes looking for me. I don't know if he'd search this far, but I'm not taking any more chances when it comes to him. I ignore the hunger growing in my belly; if I can survive however many days in the oubliette with no food, I can last a few more hours, or however long it takes me to get home. I continue walking, keeping myself as shielded from the road as possible.

My feet ache, and I'm beyond exhausted by the time I finally crest the hill and see the house Mom and I shared with Gregory. His car is outside, and the front gate is swinging open in the light breeze. Nothing seems to have changed. I slip into the back-yard and peek through the kitchen window. There doesn't seem to be any sign of life inside, but that means nothing with Gregory. He's probably paralytic from his latest drinking spree and upstairs in bed, even at this time of the day, or he's out buying more booze.

Moving closer to the back door, I stay alert to any sudden appearance from him. I really don't want to get caught after making it so far. Gregory's temper frightens me, but it's nothing compared to my daddy's. Everything Pater does is executed with a clear head, and the outcome is always *exactly* as he wants it to be; his utter conviction and calculated responses make him far more terrifying than Gregory, but a confrontation with my stepdad is always best avoided. No matter how predictable his actions, he's still a loose cannon and will lash out at the slightest thing. Gregory lacks the finesse that Pater has perfected, but comparing them makes me realize their tempers and the heavy-handed way each of them control those around them is very similar. I'd rather fly under the radar than go toe to toe with either of them.

Chapter Twenty-Five

The risk I'm about to take is stupid and reckless, it may very well land me straight back in my daddy's lap, but I don't see any other options. I don't want to be a mother to my father's children, no matter how much I've come to love him. This love is so wrong, and even though I still want it desperately, I could feel myself being dragged deeper into the tangled roots of my family the longer I stayed. I could turn around and go back, but then all of this will have been for nothing and I'll still face the same consequences. If I continue to stand here and dwell on all of the possibilities, I'm bound to get caught. I need to do this now while the coast is clear.

I twist the handle on the door and am pleased but unsurprised when it opens. We hardly ever locked it. People rarely venture this way, and it's not like we'd anything worth stealing if thieves did happen to visit. I step into the house, the familiar lingering stench of Gregory's favorite booze reaches my nose, and I scrunch it up in disgust. *Seems that hasn't changed either.*

I'm here now, and it's too late to turn tail and leave. It's strange being back. Even though it's only been a few weeks, it feels like months or even years have passed. I listen for any indication that my presence has been noticed, but all I can hear is the emptiness of the house screaming back at me, telling me I'm alone.

Avoiding the many bottles of alcohol stocked in the fridge, I grab a can of soda and then rummage through the cupboards for a bag of chips. It's not real food, but it'll tide me over for a bit until I can make something a bit more substantial. Clutching the packet in my hand, I inch cautiously farther into the house, scanning the rooms as I pass them and head for the stairs. It's eerily quiet, but I'd rather be creeped out by silence than face Gregory right now.

I manage to sneak upstairs without any difficulty, and when I wander into my bedroom, I'm pleasantly surprised he hasn't trashed it in a fit of rage. I do notice that there are a few things out of place, but I was in a hurry to get away from here last time I was in my room; I could've easily disturbed them when I was packing my bag, preparing to leave this place behind forever. *I shouldn't be here.*

Closing the door behind me, I strip back the covers on the bed, and remove the pillowcase from my pillow. As I work, small puffs of dust kick up from the layers that have built up over the weeks of disuse. Once the air has cleared, I sit down on the edge of the bed, devour the chips and gulp down my drink. It's not much, but it takes the edge off my hunger and thirst, allowing me to pay attention to how exhausted I'm feeling. I decide to risk taking a short nap, and I lie down on the bed, fully dressed, and let sleep whisk me away from my weary thoughts.

I don't know how long I've been asleep, but when I wake up my stomach is rumbling angrily at me, and I desperately need the bathroom. It's fully dark, and glancing at the clock still sitting on my nightstand, I see that it's around 1 a.m. Sitting up, I flick on the small lamp and get up, whimpering slightly at the throbbing in the soles of my feet and my aching muscles. I sneak across my bedroom and out into the hallway. As I make my way to the bathroom, I hear heavy snoring coming from my Mom's room. Gregory's home. Thankfully, when he's sleeping that soundly, not even a thunderstorm above our house will wake him.

After relieving myself, I tiptoe down the stairs to the kitchen. I can't use the stove or anything will alert him to the fact that someone else is in the house, but I can at least get some bread and make a mug of soup to take back upstairs with me. I grab my favorite mug from the back of the cupboard, careful not to make any noise, and once I've prepared my meal, I slip back upstairs to my room. My heart is pounding by the time I finally close the door, the fear of being found making it race.

Once I'm back in my room, I can finally breathe again. Gregory is less of a threat to me than Pater, but I still feel on edge not knowing how he'd react to me being in the house. We didn't exactly part on good terms when I left here, or when I fled his crazy momma's house. *Why did I think coming back here was a good idea?*

It's too late now to reconsider the idiocy of my decision, but then again, the choice was between Gregory and his temper, or Pater and his determination to start a family with me. *Not much of a choice, either way.* Shaking my head, I take a seat at my desk and break off a piece of bread before dipping it into the soup and taking a bite. The strong flavor of the hot tomato soup is delicious, and it doesn't take me long to demolish the bread and drain the mug completely. Feeling satisfied and a lot better than I did when I awoke, I set the empty mug down.

Moving over to the bed, I scoop up my backpack, and empty everything out onto the bed. Bypassing the envelope that contains all the secrets I unearthed about my heritage, I rifle through the remaining photographs until I find the one of my mom and me, and I pick it up. Brushing a finger over the glossy surface, I gaze at our happy faces for a long time. Now I can see clearly the hint of sadness in her gaze as she holds me tightly to her, and I sigh wistfully as I reflect on the innocence that has been lost since this was taken, and not just at my daddy's hand.

Chapter Twenty-Six

I wake up and stretch out on my bed. The lamp is still on, and the sun is streaming faintly through the window, landing directly on my face. I realize I never drew the blinds, and I blink disoriented as I stare around my old room and glance at the clock that now reads 6:30 a.m. I don't even remember falling asleep. Then it all comes rushing back...I ran away from Pater and my family. I feel a pang of regret, even though I've woken without the accompanying stress and tension I've become used to when anticipating Pater's mood. Given that I just snuck into my old home and am now attempting to conceal my presence from Gregory, Pater should be the least of my worries.

Sitting up, I perch on the edge of my bed. A wave of dizziness comes over me, and I bend forward with my elbows resting on my knees and press my face into my palms, waiting for it to pass. When I finally feel a little better, I move over to my dresser and pull out some fresh clothes and quickly change. Resigned to being cooped up in here for the day, or at least until I know Gregory has left the house or is asleep, I stand up and move around the room, picking up and replacing my things, and trying to remove the dust that's settled in my absence.

I trip over a wire trailing across the floor and manage to stop myself falling over and making a noise. Looking down, I realize it's my phone charger. I retrieve my dead phone from my backpack and plug it in. While waiting for the battery to charge, I continue to reorganize my room.

When I eventually check back, the power bar on the screen reads 21%,and I switch my phone on. There are no missed calls or texts from anyone other than Gregory, but as I'm about to lock the screen, I see something that makes me pause. I stare in disbelief at the small electronic screen that informs me it's been nearly three months since I ran away from home. *I don't even know how to process that. Three months?* My mind is racing as I attempt to work out how so much time can have passed, but I come up blank. *How can three months have come and gone, when it feels like only a few weeks have passed?*

I feel sick with the knowledge that I've lost so much time. I've been consumed with everything that's been going on at my daddy's house and the routine I'd settled into, and it didn't seem so long. I'm at a complete loss. Looking around my room, it now makes sense why everything was so dusty before I cleaned in here this morning. Another bout of dizziness comes over me. My stomach roils, and as the nausea hits, I lean forward, feeling like I'm going to throw up.

Gradually, my head begins to clear, but the unsettled feeling in my stomach lingers. The conversation I had with Jocelyn filters into my mind, and I cover my mouth with my hand. *No, no, no!* Tears start to fall down my face, and wrapping my arms around my stomach, I fight back the sobs that threaten to break out. If Gregory hears me crying, he'll come to investigate and find me. I don't want to think about what he'll do, especially if he learns I might be carrying Pater's child.

No, I'm not pregnant, I can't be. I refuse to entertain that possibility. Like I told Jocelyn, it's not unusual for me to be late, so I'm probably just PMSing right now. But the problem with PMSing is that when I finally do start my cycle, I won't have ready access to a bathroom. I straighten up, and wipe the tears from my cheeks. I have to pull myself together. Breathing deeply, I do my best to assess the situation while waiting for my stomach to settle. I've no money left, limited access to food and drink, and there's an incredibly high likelihood that Gregory will discover me hiding in the house. Plus, I'm almost certain I have an extremely angry daddy who's wondering where I've run off to and waiting for an opportunity to drag me back to his house. *I'm so fucked.*

I spend the rest of the day pottering around the bedroom, waiting for Gregory to either leave on a beer run or go to bed so I can slip out to use the bathroom and scavenge more food from the fridge and cupboards. I didn't find my abandoned sleeping bag or tent in my room, but I may be able to locate them in the house if Gregory goes out for long enough. Not that they'll do me much good at this point, but if I do need to run again, at least I'll have something warm to sleep in at night.

At around 7 p.m. I hear the sound of the front door opening and closing and then Gregory's car starting. Seizing the small window of opportunity, I grab my empty backpack and rush downstairs to the kitchen. Opening the cupboards I grab some cans of food that I know Gregory won't touch, containing stuff like fruit and mac and cheese, and I gather a few other things that Mom had bought for me. I smile when I think about how she'd always complain about how quickly I'd finish them off. *I wish she was here.* Burying my emotions, I shove as many items in my bag as I can manage without making it too heavy to carry, and then I sprint back up to my room.

I've barely closed my door when the front door bursts open and Gregory comes into the house, slamming the door shut behind him before storming up the stairs. *Shit! Does he know I'm here?* I scurry across to my bed, and crawling underneath it, I hide, petrified. My heart is thundering in my chest with the terror that maybe he's discovered I'm here, but he rushes straight past and into his room, shutting the door behind him with enough force to rattle the windows. I wait perfectly still, lying flush against the carpet, waiting for my nerves to settle and too afraid to move in case he hears me and comes to investigate.

I should never have left Pater's house; under his roof I knew what to expect, but this is almost unbearable. I've been reduced to hiding beneath my bed, trying to remain undetected while my stepdad goes on a furious rampage through the house. When I finally feel calm enough, I slide out from under the bed, brush myself off and let the tears fall. *What am I going to do?*

Chapter Twenty-Seven

The next morning, I wake up in a cold sweat, with nausea ripping painfully through me. Not stopping to second guess my actions, I slide out of bed and dash for the bathroom with one hand over my mouth and the other clutching my stomach. Bursting into the bathroom, I shut the door and fumble for the light switch before lunging for the toilet and emptying the contents of my stomach into it. I don't know how long I'm there, sweating and shivering in between bouts of vomiting, but I'm vaguely aware of the door opening, and a figure standing in the doorway, casting a shadow over my shaking body.

"What the fuck are you doing here, Fia?" Gregory exclaims in shock, and I stare blearily up at him for a moment before leaning back over the toilet.

"What do you think I'm doing here, Gregory?" I cough, feeling too crappy to care right now that my cover is blown.

Standing up, I flush and then wash my hands, before I grab a fresh toothbrush from the cupboard and start brushing my teeth to get rid of the vile taste in my mouth. When I'm done, I turn to leave the room, but Gregory is blocking my path.

"You're not leaving this room until you explain what you're doing here," he snaps, frowning at me.

I laugh weakly. "You're not my real daddy. You can't make me tell you anything."

Too late, I realize my poor choice of words as Gregory's expression clouds with anger.

"I'm your stepdad, and even though your mom isn't around anymore, you still answer to me, Fia," he growls, taking a step toward me.

I back away, suddenly wary. His words are clearly spoken, and his eyes aren't clouded with the drunken haze I'm used to seeing.

"I found him," I admit, hoping to stop him from advancing.

He pauses, his eyebrow raised, and though Gregory looks nothing like my real daddy, it reminds me vividly of Pater and the way he'd look at me. I wait with bated breath for my stepdad to respond while trying to gauge if I can slip past him and out of here before he can stop me.

Gregory looks at me thoughtfully for a moment,

and then he starts chuckling, but he doesn't sound amused; instead, he sounds bitter.

"Is that what this is?" he asks, gesturing at the toilet, and I stare at him, bewildered, waiting for him to elaborate. "What the fuck is in those genes of his that means he's able to keep spawning all these kids as fucked up as he is?"

I don't answer, because it doesn't seem like he's expecting a response. Instead, I slowly inch forward in the hopes I can make a break for it before he goes off on one of his tirades and lashes out.

"You're pregnant aren't you, and the baby is his, isn't it? Little Fia Richards is knocked up with her daddy's kid," he laughs.

"I'm not pregnant," I tell him, hoping that if I deny it out loud, it can't ever be true.

He takes a step closer, and I move back reflexively, hitting the wall.

"Oh, you most certainly are," he hisses, and I fight not to gag as his putrid breath reaches my face.

I'm trapped between Gregory and the wall, and I've got no way to escape him now. I slap his hands away when he cups my breasts.

"These are bigger, and your hips are softer than they were when I last saw you, tied up in my momma's spare room," he says in a husky voice, squeezing my hips as he moves closer until there's no space between us, and I have no room to maneuver my way out.

"Stop it!" I scream in his face, struggling to break free of his grip.

"Your mom was so fucking sexy when she was carrying you, all flushed and swollen with *his* baby. It was one of the few times she let me fuck her," he growls, digging his fingers into my skin, and I almost throw up all over again when I feel his cock digging into my pelvis.

"Let me go!" I shout, and I lift my knee, aiming to nail him in the balls, but he traps it between his legs.

I reach up to hit him in the face, and manage to land a blow across his jaw. It does very little, though, because I can't put any momentum behind it while I'm being pinned against the bathroom wall of my childhood home.

"So full of fire, Fia," he moans, rolling his hips against me, and I let out a sob. There's no one to stop him here, and I can only hope he gets a limp dick again when it comes to acting out whatever fantasy is running through his head right now.

"Stop calling me that," I bite out, still hating how sleazy he makes the nickname sound.

"Sofia," he says, drawing out my name, and somehow that's almost worse.

I let out a sigh of relief when he backs up, releasing me. I bolt for the door, but he doesn't let me get far. I find myself being dragged back and shoved up against the same wall he just released me from with my face and front pressed against the cold tiles. Gregory's hand is planted firmly between my shoulder blades, keeping me in place. I attempt to twist away from his groping hands as he drags my leggings and panties down to my knees. I'm screaming as loud as I can, but he ignores me, jamming his fingers into my pussy and then dragging them back to where no one, not even Pater, has touched.

"Wonder how your daddy will react when he finds out I've had you too, hmm?"

"No, no, no, no, no!" I cry, over and over, when he tears into my ass with his fingers, ripping me apart.

Gregory withdraws them, and I feel the pain radiating through me and see the stickiness of blood coating his fingers from where he's brutally torn the delicate skin. He presses himself against me, and I can feel his hard, jutting cock. I close my eyes, praying for someone to save me, but no one does. My shrieks deafen me when he penetrates me, and then everything goes black.

Chapter Twenty-Eight

Pain is the only thing I can feel as I slowly come back to my senses. My ass feels as though it's been through a meat grinder, and I'm slumped over on the bathroom floor with tears clinging to my eyelashes and soaking my cheeks. I tilt my head back to look up at Gregory who is sitting on the edge of the bath, wearing a filthy, smug expression. Nausea twists my gut and I lunge for the toilet again. Lifting the lid, I vomit until my face is coated in a fresh layer of sweat, and I'm dry heaving through my racking sobs.

I jerk back to throw his hand off when he lays it on my shoulder, squeezing it as though he can offer me comfort when he's the cause of my agony and anguish.

"Your mom didn't cry this much when I fucked her ass, but then again, she wasn't a virgin there like you were. So nice and tight," he says, leaning forward and sweeping my hair from my sweaty face.

"Don't touch me," I reply hoarsely, flinching away from his touch.

Ignoring me, he lifts my hair and pries the damp strands away from my cheeks. Then rubbing salt in the wound he's created, he grabs a washcloth, runs it under the faucet, and wrings it out before offering it to me. I slap it out of his hand with a glare, and it makes a wet sound as it hits the tiled floor beside me

"Fuck you!" I spit out, putting as much hate and venom into my tone as I can muster.

"Maybe later. I'm not as young as I used to be," he replies, and I recoil in disgust.

"You're disgusting. Get out!" I shout, jerking my hand toward the door, wishing he'd leave me in peace.

"You'll give it up for him, but not for me." he says, injecting false sadness into his tone.

"I don't know what you're talking about," I deny, but as always, his barbs sting.

"Like fuck you don't. You didn't even bother trying to hide the fact that the baby you're carrying is his until I stuck my dick in you just now. Did your daddy turn you on?" he asks slyly.

"Stop it!" I scream, and his smirk deepens.

"I bet he did. Luke got you all wet and slick for him, and then he stuck his dick in you and filled you up with his cum didn't he? Over and over again, and you laid down and took it like a good little girl, just for him," he taunts and I can feel my heart cracking.

I pick up the nearest object and launch it at his face, but he blocks it, sending it clattering into the bathtub. I slowly stand on shaking legs, wincing as my throbbing ass stings with the movement.

"Does Luke know you're pregnant?" he asks.

"You're not a doctor, so you can fuck off with your assumptions," I snap.

"You're right, I'm not. But this pregnancy test should reveal all. While you were enjoying your little beauty sleep just then, I went and grabbed this from your Mom's medicine cabinet in our bedroom. She was always so worried I'd get her pregnant with my kid, so she used to keep a test handy, just in case. I'm sure you can figure out how to take it."

He holds it out to me, and I take it with shaking hands and then throw it straight back at him. His yell of surprise and pain when the corner of the box jabs him in the eye gives me a small sense of satisfaction, but it doesn't even come close to repaying him for the agony he just inflicted on my body.

"Go fuck yourself," I snarl, kicking my leg out and catching him straight in the balls before shoving him into the bathtub.

Gregory's angry shout follows me as I flee the bathroom and sprint down the hallway to my room, ignoring my body as it protests against the sudden intense movement. Throwing the door open, I grab my empty backpack and shove everything into it I can reach. I'm about to turn and leave when I see Gregory standing in my doorway with fury written all over his face.

"Where the hell do you think you're going, Sofia?" he demands, prowling toward me

"I'm not staying here with you," I scoff, eyeing up the open door behind him and praying I can make it through before he catches me.

"Do you really think it'll be better for you there with him? What about when he finds out you're carrying his baby? I can't imagine he'll be too happy to learn you ran off with his unborn child like your mom did, especially as you ended up coming back here to *me*."

"I didn't come back to *you*. You weren't supposed to know I was even here!" I yell at him.

Gregory moves closer, and I back away, "Stay the fuck away from me." I scream at the top of my lungs when he grabs me, "GET YOUR FILTHY HANDS OFF ME!"

"You know what. How about we find out, shall we? I think maybe he'll thank me for bringing his fucking spawn home to him. Wait 'til he finds out what I've got to tell him" he jeers, and my heart freezes at his threat.

If Pater gets hold of me, I'm certain he'll throw me down that hole again just for running away. I don't even want to contemplate how he'll react if he believes Gregory's right about me and thinks I knowingly ran away carrying his baby. *What will he do to me?*

"Let go! Stop!" I shriek, struggling weakly against him and trying to nail him in the groin again.

"Nope, you're coming with me. I'm not putting up with this. Kayley always behaved herself until she fucked off to her grave and left me with you, but you won't do as you're fucking told, so you can go home to the man I *know* will make you obey. At least, I got my piece of you first," he smirks.

"I hope he rips your fucking dick off," I snap, thrashing in his hold and trying desperately to get free.

If there's one thing I've learned, it's that Pater loves his children, even if he expresses it in a completely screwed up way, and I'm his blood. I just hope he remembers that when he sees me again. Gregory drags me out to his car, and opening the rear passenger door, he pushes me inside and engages the child lock so I can't jump out while he makes his way around to the driver's side. I don't sit still and behave. I wrench off a headrest and start slamming the metal prongs against the window, trying to break the glass. He opens the rear door again and snatches the headrest out of my hands, hurling it away into the bushes. I scratch him across the face and kick out at him, but he pins me down and fixes me with his angry glare. The mania in his eyes makes me pause, and I wonder how much further I can push him before he snaps and does something I won't recover from. My body will heal, and the mental scars will eventually fade, but I can't come back from death if he were to strangle the life from my body.

"Sit still and fucking be quiet," he hurls at me, and I cower back in the seat.

Realizing there's no way to escape the fate approaching me, I stop fighting. But Gregory is mistaken if he thinks for one second I'm going to keep obeying him and stay docile. When we get back to Pater's house, I'm going to kick him down that fucking hole myself.

Gregory starts the car and begins to drive, muttering under his breath and occasionally growling about how it would serve Luke right if I didn't make it back to him.

"This is for the best. Besides, I'm not raising another one of Luke's brats, especially if it turns out to be anything like *you*," he throws over his shoulder, giving me a hateful stare.

I don't give him the satisfaction of answering. Instead, I shuffle around to try and get comfortable so I'm not putting all my weight on my ass. This is not the best outcome for me, and I'm terrified of what awaits me at the end of this journey. I'm not sure what else fate has in store for me, but I'm not going to say another word to Gregory. All I can hope is that Pater destroys him before I receive my punishment, so I can watch him get what he deserves.

The drive to Pater's house takes no more than an hour, and I can feel Gregory's eyes on me almost the entire time, making my skin crawl. Something changed in him after Mom died. He was never nice, but he's more of a monster now than he ever was before.

"Ready to face him, Fia?" he asks, stopping the engine and turning in his seat to look at me.

"I'd rather face him than spend another minute with you," I sneer, sounding a lot braver than I feel.

Chapter Twenty-Nine

Fear makes my heart skitter at the sight of Pater's house, and I wring my hands together in my lap. Gregory doesn't give me a chance to brace myself for what's coming, though. As soon as he exits the car, he opens the rear passenger door and starts to pull me out by my arm. I throw myself across the seat, attempting to climb through to the front passenger side door, but I barely get my fingers wrapped around the handle before I'm being dragged from the car, this time by my ankles.

I land on my ass on the driveway and let out a howl when pain shoots through my body. The sound of the front door hitting the wall as it's yanked open distracts Gregory for a moment, and I scramble away on my hands and knees to hide behind his car. I want to get as far away from him as possible, so he can't hurt me or use me as his shield against Pater's wrath. There's no way I'll come out of this unscathed, but I'm not going down with Gregory. If I can get away from here I will, but in my current state, the chances of that are slim to none.

"Well, well, look what came crawling up my driveway," Pater drawls, sounding surprised.

I can see the cool facade he's wearing as he steps out into the sunlight.

"Luke," Gregory acknowledges, but Pater doesn't respond. Instead, he waits for him to continue. "I brought back something that belongs to you," Gregory says, speaking as casually as though he'd brought back a borrowed object, rather than the stepdaughter he raised and recently raped in her mom's house.

"Oh, and what might that be?" Pater responds, crossing his arms over his chest and raising an eyebrow, "Doesn't look like you've got shit for me in that piece of crap car of yours, Greg."

"Where the fuck has she gone?" Gregory exclaims, walking back to where he'd left me sprawled in the dirt.

My lungs are constricted with panic, and I can't move from my spot behind the car. He's going to find me, any second now. I'm already in Pater's line of sight.

"Well, why don't you go, and come back later when you've figured out what bullshit was important enough to disturb my morning," Pater says disparagingly, cocking his head to one side, eyes now fixed on me, and with a dark gleam in them promising retribution for what I've done.

"Your brat came crawling back to me. She broke into my home and assaulted me," Gregory snaps, "And don't fucking talk to me like I'm one of those kids of yours."

"Watch your mouth when you talk about my kids and don't try and order me around like I'm a piece of shit. I'm gonna talk to you however I fucking like," Pater sneers back at him, and his dark eyes flicker in my direction again.

He knows I'm here, but he's either waiting for me to come forward, or for Gregory to stop fucking around and spit out the rest of his string of bullshit. Gregory is stalling, and I can see the sweat on the back of his neck and his hands shaking. The show he's been putting on with me is a load of false bravado because right now, face to face with Luke Greene, he's pissing his damn pants.

"So which of my kids do you think you've brought home to me then, Greg?" Pater gets straight to the point, no doubt already fed up with Gregory's pussyfooting around.

"Kayley's little girl, Sofia Richards," my stepdad snaps back.

The scowl that crosses Pater's face in that moment is terrifying, and his tone is heavy with threat when he utters, "*Greene.*"

Gregory shakes his head, "Kayley had her last name legally changed when the kid was born. She's Sofia Richards."

"I don't give a damn what her legal name is, she's a Greene and she belongs to *me*."

I gasp, and Gregory looks back over his shoulder, this time spotting me crouched behind the car. I yelp when he lunges for me and grabs me by the wrist, dragging me across the dirt and throwing me at my daddy's feet. I twist as I fall, landing heavily on my side, and I grunt when the ground jars my body as I connect with it. I look fearfully up at Pater, yet I can't ignore the warmth that flows through me at the sight of him. I feel safer in his presence than I ever did with Gregory, and that's so fucked up.

"She's just like her mother, came crawling back to me when you were done with her," he taunts, and I watch Pater's expression as it darkens, and his eyes turn black.

"I wasn't *done* with Kayley. She lied and said she'd had a miscarriage when really she was still pregnant with my child. *You* covered it up and helped her get away, and now you have the fucking nerve to come back here and throw my daughter, who *you* helped Kayley hide from me, at my goddamn feet."

"I'm not the only one who's been keeping secrets, am I, Fia?" Gregory snaps.

"Don't fucking call me that!" I screech at him, scrambling to get to my feet.

I move to take a step toward him, but a pair of arms wrap around me, and I'm pulled flush against the solid chest of my daddy.

"What secrets have you been keeping from me now, Fia?" Pater growls in my ear, and I shiver against him

"I found her puking in my bathroom this morning. Your little girl is fucking pregnant, Luke. Congratulations, you're gonna be a daddy again."

Chapter Thirty

A deathly silence falls after Gregory's terrible revelation, and I feel Pater's arms tighten around me at his words.

"I don't even know if that's true," I whisper, hoping he'll believe me.

"I'll deal with you later, after I've taken care of this," he growls in my ear, then refocuses his attention on Gregory who looks a bit dismayed that he didn't get a bigger reaction out of Pater.

The explosion is coming, but Pater will unleash his anger on me in private, and not where Gregory can gloat at his leisure. He's not getting any more pain out of me, not now, not ever.

"She's in denial. She even refused to take a pregnancy test when I gave her one. She just threw it back in my face!" he shouts.

I snap, and scream back at him, "You fucking

raped me and then thought I would do as you told me! You're out of your goddamn mind, so yeah, I threw it back at you. I hope you rot in fucking hell for what you put me through!"

I dissolve into tears, collapsing to the ground at Pater's feet when he slowly releases me from his iron grip. I look up at him through hazy eyes and watch as he walks past where I'm sitting on the ground. Even with the watery blur obscuring my vision, there's no mistaking the expression on his face for anything other than murderous.

I wipe my eyes just in time to see Pater swing a fist at Gregory and nearly knock him over with a single blow. Gregory moans and backs away, trying to escape from the onslaught he knows is coming. Pater lashes out again, punching him in the jaw, and I see Gregory spit out a mouthful of blood while continuing to move back as my daddy advances on him.

"I'll fucking kill you for touching my daughter. You knew who she belonged to, and *still*, you touched what's not yours. Not only that, but you fucked her momma *and* helped her keep my baby girl away from me for eighteen years," Pater thunders, before cocking his head to one side and shaking it at Gregory in mock disbelief. "I'm going to enjoy *this* very much."

Gregory manages to open his car door, but Pater kicks it closed. An ear-splitting scream rends the air, and my stomach turns when I see Gregory yank open the door and lift his now completely mangled hand free. I feel sick, but I'm also mesmerized by what I'm seeing, and I wonder what's wrong with me that I can't muster any semblance of sympathy for my stepdad.

Pater lands another hit, sending Gregory reeling. Then, without giving him a chance to recover, he kicks him solidly in the shin, and I cringe when I hear the crack of bone. Dark fury is fueling my daddy, and I know better than to try and stop him. All I can do is watch helplessly with my hand over my mouth to keep the scream from escaping.

Pater continues to pummel and beat Gregory to a pulp until my stepdad's face is almost completely unrecognizable as human anymore. Horror and disgust rip through me, and I have to swallow hard to keep from throwing up when my stomach rebels against the sight in front of me.

My daddy is savage, lethal, and terrifyingly glorious in this moment. His complete dominance and power fill me with awe. I try to convince myself I'm not enjoying watching Gregory on the ground, spluttering, bleeding, and spitting up blood... but disturbingly, I am. Pater straightens, and looks at me, smirking when he sees my expression. His face is splattered with blood; red speckles coat his white shirt, and I can see his fists are dripping with blood when he stops for a split-second. Even after exerting himself, his heavy breaths are slow, and I wonder what kind of demon he must be, to be able to hold such control over himself when he's beaten a man nearly to death.

"Please, stop" Gregory wheezes, raising his mangled hand in surrender.

"Are you giving up, Gregory? Have you had enough now, and you want me to stop?" Pater inquires mockingly, crouching down to look at him.

"Yes, please," he begs.

Pater looks over at me. I'm still sitting, frozen in place, where he left me.

"Fia, baby, tell me. Did you beg him to stop when he fucked you against your will?"

I stare at him, not answering, and he stands up, sighing impatiently.

"Answer me! Did you beg him to stop when he put his *filthy* dick in your body?"

"Yes, Daddy," I whisper, and he nods, looking down at the whimpering mess of a man at his feet.

"And did he stop when you begged him to?" he asks, and a fresh stream of tears rolls down my cheeks as I shake my head in response.

"Did you hear that, Greg? You're asking me to stop, even though you didn't grant my daughter mercy when she *begged* and *pleaded* with you to stop fucking her. So, why don't *you* answer me on this, Greg? Why the *fuck* should I stop?"

Pater brings up his foot and stamps down on

Gregory's broken hand, and the sounds of flesh and leather connecting, bones crunching, and the splatter of blood and tissue make me retch. Then, he stamps down on Gregory's groin, rendering his foul cock useless, and proceeds to drag him around the back of the house. Awkwardly, I get back onto my feet and follow them, being careful not to step on the small trails of blood that Gregory leaves behind. *What's Pater going to do now?*

I tentatively keep a few steps behind and continue to let them lead me around the house until we get to the backyard. I linger a few meters away, afraid to leave and afraid to stay, but something keeps me here, watching everything unfold. Pater releases Gregory, letting him slump on the ground where he lies moaning and jerking feebly. He's a complete mess, but I can tell that Pater isn't anywhere near done with him yet. Fear spikes my heart; there's more anger emanating from my daddy than I've ever seen before.

He kicks Gregory in the gut, winding him, and then drops down onto one knee beside him, leaning in low and speaking slowly but clearly.

"You're not good enough to be a father, but don't worry I'll take it from here. I'm gonna keep on going. Because you know what, Greg? Just because *you're* done, doesn't mean I am."

I can just about make out Gregory's pained expression beneath the damage, blood, and tears distorting his face. He's trying to crawl away from Pater, but with his mangled hand and my daddy holding him in place, he's trapped and completely at his mercy. The trouble is Pater will give him none, just like Gregory refused to give me any when he was holding me down and raping the last scrap of innocence from me.

"Fia, get over here, baby girl," Pater orders, lifting Gregory to his feet and punching him again. When I don't move, he sighs impatiently.

"Fia, now!" he demands more harshly.

Biting my lip, I move closer to him, but still standing just out of reach. He releases Gregory who crumples to the ground while weakly trying to curl himself in a protective ball. Pater stands and walks toward me. I take an automatic step back, but stop when his eyes flash with a warning I can't ignore.

"Finish him off," he orders, and I gape up at him, "Don't stand there with your mouth open like that unless you want it filled. Now, do as you're told and kill him."

Chapter Thirty-One

I can't believe he's asking me to deal the final blow and end Gregory's life. I move slowly forward, hating that every step brings me closer to the man I'm about to kill. I don't even know what to do, yet my daddy expects this of me. I'm losing myself, more and more, and I don't know who I'm going to be at the end of this.

I stand next to the pitiful excuse of a man weeping and groaning on the ground at my feet, and I see the blood seeping out of his wounds caused by my daddy's fists. He deserved every single one of those. *Is letting him live after all of this really a mercy, or would killing him be kinder? Should I offer him the mercy he denied me and has been denied him in return? How do I decide whether or not to cross the line between innocence and murder?*

I make my decision, and inhaling a shaky

breath, I cringe as I approach Gregory the man who violated my body just hours ago. I loosen the buckle of the belt, and I whip it free, startling myself when it cuts through the air. I glance toward Pater who has taken a few steps back and is watching with a smile on his lips.

I surrender to it, to the dark side of me that belongs to Pater, and I slash the belt down, bringing it across Gregory's bare ass, making him howl in fresh pain. Fighting back the fear over what I'm about to do, I send it flying again. I don't have the strength to keep on doing this, so I climb onto his back, and wrapping the thick band of leather around his neck, I loop it through the buckle. I look again to my daddy for guidance and approval. It's not in me to draw this out like he would.

Pater nods and I pull it tight, slowly choking the life from the man beneath me. This time I'm in control, and his life is in my hands. Gregory gags and chokes as he tries to reach back to dislodge me, but I don't let go, and I don't loosen the improvised noose I've created from metal and leather. The skin of his neck above the belt is turning blotchy, purpling from the lack of oxygen. I'm killing him with my own two hands. Soon he stops moving, but I keep my position while my hands shake and tears fall down my face.

At this moment, I know exactly who I am. Luke Greene is my daddy, and I'm his daughter. Sofia

Richards is gone; she's dead, just like her mother, and Sofia Greene has taken up residence in her place.

I slide off him, stumbling in my urgency to get away from the beaten, bruised, bloody, and completely broken corpse now lying in the center of our backyard. I let out a surprised yelp when Pater reaches out and grabs my arm, pulling me toward him and kissing me deeply. He steals my breath, and wraps his hands around me, staining me with blood.

"You did very well there, Fia. For a moment I wasn't sure you had it in you. I'm just going to take care of this piece of shit. You're gonna go and get yourself cleaned up, and then you've got some explaining to do. Don't even dare to think about running again."

"Yes, Daddy," I mumble.

Darting into the house, I hurry down the hallway to my bedroom, hoping that I still have some clothes here. I nearly shriek when I walk in and see Jocelyn sitting on the bed, leveling me with a serious look.

"I heard what Gregory said about you. I *knew* you were pregnant. I *told* you to take the test!" she whisper-yells at me, and I glance nervously over my shoulder.

"I don't know if what he said was true. I never took the test you showed me or the one he gave me," I admit, biting my lip.

"We need to find out. Pater is going to want to know, and you better have some answers for him when he asks."

I nod, and swallow the lump in my throat. Jocelyn hands me some fresh clothes, and I take them with a murmured, "Thanks."

"I'll be here if you need me," Jocelyn says as I turn to leave the room.

"Thank you," I whisper again, smiling faintly as I leave the room.

I hurry along to the bathroom, and slip inside, locking the door behind me. The cupboard where Jocelyn retrieved the test from seems to be staring at me, but I turn my back on it and strip before getting the water running for a shower. I don't have time to linger and relax beneath the hot water, so I carefully scrub myself clean, gingerly washing around my tender ass. I hiss as the suds run down, stinging the split skin. Tears fall, mingling with the water as I try to delay the inevitable. The guilt for what I did rips at my soul, and the worst part is I don't feel sad about Gregory's death. Now he'll never be able to come back and haunt me, except maybe in my nightmares.

I sigh heavily, and stepping out of the shower, I wrap a towel around my body and start to dry myself. Bruises coat my body, some just starting to blossom, and others old and fading, all showing more vividly now that the layer of filth and blood has been washed away. I slowly dress, and with my heart in my mouth, I retrieve the pregnancy test that Jocelyn has stashed in the little cupboard. I try not to think about why she has it, and why I'm about to use it.

Minutes later the result is ready, but I'm too afraid to look. A soft knocking on the bathroom door snags my attention, distracting me from my chaotic thoughts. It must be Jocelyn. Opening it, I'm unsurprised and grateful for her presence. I let her in and her eyes lock on the test still sitting by the washbasin.

"Well?" she asks expectantly, and I guiltily screw up my face.

"I don't know. I haven't looked yet. I'm afraid of what the answer will be. Though, I guess in a way I already know what it's going to say. I just can't bring myself to face it," I admit, letting out a shuddery breath.

"You can't put it off forever. Look at it," she urges.

Twisting my hands, I let out a groan and pick up the test. My hands are shaking, and my heart feels like it's going to break through my rib cage, it's beating so hard and fast. I look at the little window and the plastic testing stick slides out of my hand, hitting the floor

I glance up at Jocelyn and whisper, "Positive. I'm pregnant."

She picks it up and looks at it to confirm before dropping it in the trash. She washes her hands and I follow suit, and when I'm done, she pulls me into her arms.

I can feel her shaking against me as she whispers, "I'm so sorry. I was hoping for your sake it wouldn't be positive."

I laugh hollowly. "Me too. Thanks for being here with me."

"We're family, and you needed me. I wouldn't be anywhere else."

Chapter Thirty-Two

I leave the bathroom, feeling like I've got a lead weight in my stomach instead of a baby. Walking down the hallway I try not to imagine I'm heading toward a firing squad; although, if I were, at least the outcome would be a predictable one. I ran away when I was unknowingly carrying his child. I'll be lucky if he forgives me, but I'm foolishly hoping that maybe he'll be less inclined to punish me at the risk of hurting his unborn baby.

I'm burdened with the knowledge of what resides within me. I know in my heart it's wrong, yet somehow I want it anyway. That conviction carries me forward, even though the survival instinct in me is hollering at the top of its lungs for me to turn tail and run. I've nowhere to run to, though, and when my only other living relative learns what has become of her son, she'll wish nothing but harm upon me too.

I'm trying so hard to keep myself composed. Knowing what Pater has given me, and what I'm going to give him in return, I want to shed the heavy weight of despair I'm carrying and exchange it for a feeling of happiness. But my mind rebels at the possibility of him loving his unborn son or daughter in the way he loves me. I push that thought from my mind, bringing my focus back to the here and now. I've got to survive whatever's coming for me first.

The family room is empty when I arrive. Gregory's body is no longer lying in there, but his blood still stains the flooring. I'm just about to take a seat on the couch when Pater bellows loud enough for the whole house to hear.

"SOFIA! Get your ass upstairs, we're going to have a little chat."

I stop in my tracks, gulping down the lump in my throat that refuses to shift. Whatever he has planned for me, he wants it to be private, and he wants everyone to know I'm in deep fucking water with him right now. My cheeks heat as I make my way out of the room and up the stairs, recalling what happened last time I was up there. I somehow doubt this will be the same...but then again, with *him*, who knows what he's got planned.

My palms are sweaty and my hands begin to

shake the closer I get to the second floor. All the doors are shut, apart from one, just like they were last time. Pater is leaning with his shoulder against the doorframe of his bedroom with a hard to read expression on his face. I'm not sure what awaits me in there, whether good or bad, all I know is it'll be delivered by Pater. Steeling myself as best I can, I approach him while trying not to look nervous. But, if his predatory grin is anything to go by, I'm completely failing.

Drawing closer to him, I see his golden-brown eyes darken until they're nearly black. My breaths are coming more rapidly, and I fist my hands at my sides to try and control the shaking. I walk past him and into the bedroom. He closes the door behind me and locks it, every click resounding in my eardrums like gunshots. I'm more tense now than when he interrogated me and took my virginity, and I'm more on edge than when he asked me to come up here the first time, and on that occasion, I wasn't in trouble with him or preparing to receive a punishment.

I don't realize I've stopped moving until I see Pater walk past me and sit down on the bed. He doesn't say anything, and I know he's waiting to see if I'll have the guts to move closer. Not wanting to let him down any more than I know I have already, I close the distance until I'm standing in front of him. Even sitting, he somehow manages to tower over me, or at least, it seems that way because of his intimidating and all consuming presence.

"Sit down, and start talking, Sofia. You've got something you need to say and make sure you skip the bullshit. I'm not in the mood to hear excuses."

"I'm sorry, Daddy. I shouldn't have run and disobeyed you. I broke my promise to you when I did. I swear, I don't know why Gregory said what he said. He made a snap judgement when he found me throwing up in that bathroom. I wasn't about to take any damn test he offered me, not after what he did to me. He hurt me, Daddy. He shut me in the bathroom, pinned me against the tiles, and he raped me. I couldn't stop him." I cover my mouth with my hand to stifle my sobs, and my tears flow freely, soaking my skin.

"So you're telling me that you didn't run away from here while knowingly carrying my child. You didn't even suspect just a tiny bit that it was a possibility, when I've filled you up with my dick and cum on more than one occasion? It didn't even cross your mind? I find that very hard to believe, and I'll be honest with you, Sofia, you've given me very little reason to take your word for it," Pater says in a hard voice, fixing me with a steely stare.

"I swear, I didn't know. I wouldn't have run away if I did. I didn't know before, but-but I do now," I stammer, wiping my face, and looking up at him.

Pater raises an eyebrow expectantly, indicating I should continue and to hurry up about it.

"I took a test downstairs in the bathroom when I was getting cleaned up, and it was positive...I'm pregnant," I finally admit, somehow keeping my voice steady during the terrible revelation that will bind me even further to Pater and my family.

I wait with bated breath for his response, watching him closely for any change in his expression.

"You've made me a very proud father, Fia. You've been a good girl by doing what I've asked of you today when you killed Gregory, and even better you're giving me a baby. I think that calls for a celebration, don't you?"

Pater smiles, and his eyes search mine for a moment before he leans forward and kisses me firmly on the lips. Reaching over me, he slides his hands beneath my thighs and lifts me onto his lap so I'm straddling him. Surprise renders me speechless, but when he assaults my neck with his mouth, I moan deeply and automatically tilt my head back.

"There's my good, sweet girl, Fia," he growls.

When he palms my ass and pulls me closer, I can feel the thick erection that's tenting his pants, and I let out a soft cry of pain as my ass throbs, reminding me again of what Gregory did to me there.

Pater grabs hold of my t-shirt and rips it off me,

discarding it on the floor. He continues to ravage me with his mouth while pressing his palm possessively over my stomach where his baby is growing. I surrender to his touch and little whimpers escape from me at the feel of his mouth roaming over my skin.

Gripping my ass, he stands and turns to lay me down flat on my back on the large bed before divesting me of the rest of my clothing. He strips off his shirt, and dropping his pants, he exposes his cock. I barely have a moment to look before he roughly pulls me toward him and drives into me to the hilt. I let out a yelp as he stretches my pussy, filling me completely.

"That's a good girl. Now look at me and take it all, baby," he encourages, starting to move until he finds his rhythm and is pounding into me hard and fast.

His stare penetrates me as deeply as he does, and the wetness building in my pussy makes me want to scream with despair at the pleasure he's slowly unleashing. I hate myself for enjoying what he does to me and curse my continued inability to hate him. With every thrust into my body, Pater is wrenching apart my soul and revealing the darkness within, so I can view it with my wide and fearful eyes.

Chapter Thirty-Three

I lie on my daddy's bed in a daze with my legs still parted, and his warm cum slipping out of me. Pater fucked me to the point of exhaustion, taking out his exaltation at my pregnancy on my body. It's been hours since I ate, and I'm feeling the effects of it in my inability to focus, not to mention the rush of endorphins flowing through me from what just occurred.

"Get dressed, Fia," he says, and I move slowly to obey.

My entire body aches from the exertion and strain that has been put on it since I woke this morning. Once dressed, Pater scoops up my sore, pliant body into his arms and cradles me to his chest before standing. Looking up at his face, fear flits through me at warp speed when I see that the passionate pride has been replaced by a cold, stern expression. Pater is angry, and my mind sluggishly tries to work out what I've done in the past ten minutes to cause such an abrupt change.

"What's wrong?" I ask, forgetting myself and breaking yet another of his rules, but surprisingly, he answers my question.

"I may have rewarded you for giving me something I want very much, but it doesn't excuse what you did. You still ran, and you still broke the rules. It's all about trust, Sofia, and you've proven, time and time again, you can't be trusted. So, I'm going to have to take precautions," he says.

At his harsh admission I immediately start to struggle, trying to get out of his arms, but he only tightens his hold further. I don't want to go back to the oubliette and the dark, narrow captivity that awaits disobedient children at the bottom of that hole.

"Please, no, don't put me back down in the pit. I fucking swear, I won't disobey you again. I won't run away. Please, Daddy, I can't go back down there!"

"I've got something better in mind. I'm not going to risk one of my other kids being swayed to misbehave and help you out of there. No, you're going to stay up here, nice and close, where I can keep an eye on you and fuck you whenever I choose. You'll be fed, warm, and able to keep my kid safe in that belly until he or she is ready to come into the world. Then maybe, *maybe*, if you've been a good girl during that time I'll let you out, and we can do it all over again, Fia."

Confusion sweeps over me, mingled with the fear he's evoking in me. Carrying me along the hallway he sets me down but maintains a firm grip on me to stop me from running, not that I'd be foolish enough to try at this point. He proceeds to pull a set of keys from his pocket and unlocks one of the mysterious doors that none of us have ever seen behind. No one knows what lies beyond them except Pater, yet in a moment, I'll soon be privy to one of those secrets.

He opens the door, and I peer inside as curiosity gets the better of me. It's a simple room, not unlike the one I have downstairs, but there's a stark difference between this one and mine. In the corner is a simple wooden crib, and I realize in that moment exactly what he intends.

"Please don't lock me away, Daddy," I beg.

I grab his arm and stare up at his face, imploring him to reconsider. I don't want to be caged and imprisoned in this room throughout my pregnancy and probably after. Pater pries my fingers loose and pulls me into the room that's going to be mine from this point on.

"Your momma ran away from me when she was pregnant with you. After lying about her miscarriage, she then ran off with my cousin and hid you away from me. If I'd known the truth, then nothing on this earth would have kept me from finding you. Now you're here where you belong, and you're going to stay where I can keep an eye on you. I'm not letting you out of my sight, baby girl. Now, be good, and keep the noise down unless you wanna spend most of your days up here choking on my dick just to keep you quiet. Hell, I may have to do it anyway. Why waste this pretty little mouth of yours?" he says, gently running his thumb over my lips.

I'm gasping quietly. Small sobs are trapped inside me, held captive by a thread that's beginning to fray and split. He's locking me away, so I can't run from him again. I turn away, and my movement causes his thumb to swipe across my cheek, cutting a path through tears that I hadn't noticed were falling.

Pater strokes my hair, threading his fingers through the strands before fisting them in his grip, and forcing me to turn back to face him. He presses a fierce and possessive kiss against my mouth, but I'm too lost in my despair to respond until he tightens his hold, and growling against my lips, he uses his tongue to probe his way into my mouth, just as he has done to my soul. He's burrowed deep under my skin and into my body and heart, and I haven't got it in me to deny his wishes anymore. I once again surrender to his will, and he kisses me deeply until I'm dizzy and breathless.

In the haze he leaves behind when he releases me, I lose focus on everything, drifting in the emptiness within my soul. That is, until I hear the slam of the bedroom door and the click of the key in the lock, as he seals me inside this hellish prison with nothing but my aching heart and the life we created, growing slowly within my body.

Epilogue

The weeks have slowly dragged by, and with each one, my body has changed and swelled with our baby. I don't know whether Pater and I are having a girl or a boy, but my only hope is that the baby is healthy and happy.

I'm tired of the room he insists on keeping me confined to. The en suite bathroom means I don't need to be allowed out to use the toilet or keep myself clean. Once I'd stopped screaming, crying, and begging, almost daily, for him to let me out, he finally did. I treasure the rare days he allows me to wander the house and stand outside where I can feel the sun and wind on my face.

In the beginning, whenever he left the house to run errands, Vaughn or Jocelyn would sneak upstairs to talk to me through the bedroom door. Those moments were few and far between, but they helped keep me sane when the silence and loneliness would become too much to bear. Recently, it's just been Jocelyn who comes to visit me. Whenever I ask her where Vaughn is and why he hasn't been to see me, she refuses to answer and sometimes stops talking altogether. But even her silent presence on the other side of the door is a comfort.

Pater comes to see me often, bringing me food, clothes, and other necessities. His visits usually end with me on my knees and my mouth wrapped around his cock, or with him leaving me sprawled on my bed well fucked and full of his cum.

As our baby grows and I feel it move and kick, so does my love for this unborn innocent. Mom would hate that I'm trapped like she was, and I wish she was here to help me with the pregnancy. Maybe it's better that she isn't here to see me like this. I'm sure she'd be disgusted that it's Pater's child growing inside me, and horrified that I'm unable to truly hate him like she did. I'm balanced on the razor sharp edge between love and hate for the man who made me. I'm trying to fan the flames of hatred to life, and they're blooming stronger in my heart with each passing day, but no matter my feelings, I belong to him as his daughter, his wife, and soon to be mother of his child. I only hope that when our baby comes into the world, he will decide to keep me too.

Months later, I wake up moaning with pleasure

from a delicious dream to find Pater between my legs, his cock buried inside my pussy, slowly fucking me and moving in and out of my body. He presses a hand over my mouth when I let out another soft moan, and jerks his head meaningfully toward the crib where our baby boy, Tyler, is sleeping soundly. The slickness builds the longer he fucks me until he's coming hard inside me.

Pater doesn't remove his hand from my mouth and his heavy breaths blow warmly over my face as he looks deeply into my eyes. I gaze sleepily back up at him, wondering what's prompted this late night visit. He pulls out of me, and sits up. Running a finger down my face and neck, I shiver as tingles spread through me at the light touch until he closes his hand around my throat, squeezing tightly and cutting off my oxygen.

Leaning in close to me, he presses a soft kiss on my forehead and whispers, "Sorry it has to end like this, baby. But even though you've been so good lately, I still don't trust you. I've no need for kids who can't behave and do as they're told."

Tears leak from my eyes as I reach out to try and stop him, to make him let go of me so I can breathe. I stare up at him in horror at the betrayal as he slowly suffocates me with his bare hands. Turning my head as much as he'll allow I stare through the bars of the crib to where Tyler is sleeping peacefully,

"Don't worry, I'll take good care of our son. I'll raise him right, and he'll be a great man like his daddy is. Sweet dreams, Fia."

My innocent baby boy dreams on, completely unaware that merely feet away his momma is choking on her last breath at the hands of his father.

LUKE

As I cradle my son to my chest, rocking him gently to sleep, I look over at my sleeping wife whose sexy, swollen belly curves the bed sheet with the soon to be latest addition to our family. I do sometimes regret killing Fia, and I suppose it would've been ideal to have her here to look after the baby while I'm having my way with Jocelyn.

However, once she was no longer weighed down with her pregnancy, I couldn't trust her not to try to escape. Plus, with Jocelyn now free of the oubliette, there was the risk that the two of them would collaborate and succeed in doing what Jocelyn's been trying to do to me for years.

I could've kept her locked away in my rooms or down in the oubliette, but with Jocelyn now pregnant, and my young son to raise, I've no need for any other wives to breed and raise my children. Jocelyn has long since proved herself capable of being a doting and loving wife for me, and the perfect mother for our baby and my son. Fia was fiery, but Jocelyn's spark will always burn the brightest. She always has and always will come first in my heart.

THE END

Acknowledgments

Yolanda. Thank you so much for trusting me and inviting me to play in Inferno World with you and the other ladies. It was a freaking dream come true, a huge honour, and I can hardly believe it. But here it is, a whole damn novel because of you and I'm still all emotional about it. This has been incredible to do, and I'm completely overwhelmed that you let me play with Daddy and the other characters from Inferno. I'm going to leave it here before I get all weepy and feely about it all over again.
Much love, Ally x

To my awesome alpha readers Faith and Karen, and beta readers Dawn and Linda, you ladies were absolutely fantastic. Your feedback, encouragement and eagerness to devour this story was astounding.
Thank you for all your help with this, especially

making sure I didn't hold myself and the darkness back.
Keep it crazy ladies!

To my PA Renee, thank you as always for keeping me sane and keeping me on track in the midst of all of the chaos and madness in my life.

Thank you to Sheena for being ever meticulous in helping whip this into shape with your kickass editing. What would I ever do without you?

Thank you to Dez of Pretty in Ink Creations for my stunning cover, and to Abigail of Pink Elephant Designs for the gorgeous formatting.

Lastly, thank you to all the readers who went on this journey with me.

About Ally Vance

Ally is an International Bestselling Author who writes in the Dark Romance & Horror genres. Ally has been writing since she was a teenager, and it had been a long time dream of hers to finally become a published author. Ally also co-writes with her close friend Michelle under the pen name Ally Michelle. Ally lives in Kent, in the United Kingdom with her husband, stepson and two cats.

FOLLOW ALLY VANCE

Horror Reader Group:
https://bit.ly/TheDarkVault

Dark Romance Reader Group:
http://bit.ly/MayhemHearts

Newsletter:
https://bit.ly/AllyVanceNewsletter

Other Books By Ally Vance

Flower in the Dark

Just Breathe Anthology*

Evelina: Blaire's World

Fractured Darkness

Delinquent: Cavalieri Della Morte

Ignite

A Family Affair: An Extreme Taboo Anthology*

Perfect Denial (Stonewood Saga #1)

Indolence

Scream Queens: A Horror Anthology**

Mutatus: Carnaval des Ténèbres

Flagrant: An Inferno World Novel

*Denotes as Out of Print

**Anthologies are Limited Time Only Releases

Hatter & His Alice (Naughty Ever Afters #1)

In Plain Sight

Coming Soon From Ally Vance

The Society Anthology**
Another Family Affair: An Extreme Taboo
Anthology (Volume #2)**
Girls Night Anthology**
Hellfire (Stonewood Saga #2)

Printed in Great Britain
by Amazon